BREAKING FREE

The Broken Hearts Club

MICHELE BARLOW

Coffee, Friends, and Tales of Woe

Cover Design by Jacqueline Sweet

Last Page Publishing

❀ Created with Vellum

A true friend is someone who sees the pain in your eyes while everyone else believes your smile.

Luna was doing her best to control the panic attack that was building inside her chest. She was sitting in the back section at an IHOP with the women she would forever call her soul mates.

One of her friends was leaving and it felt like she had been punched in the gut. She was happy for her friend Cambry, and wanted the best for her, and it wasn't as if they wouldn't see her anymore, just not as often.

She still had Dawn, Waverly, Elena, Adalyn, Paisley, Claire, Gianna and her friend Evie and now Cambry who had moved away. The miles that separated them didn't dampen their friendship, and she hoped it never would.

The one thing that was always a constant, was

that even if people left their group, there was always someone new that needed to find solace.

Luna's purse was sitting in her lap and she could feel the vibration of her phone through the fabric. Another buzz. Text messages from her ex-husband's family. They sent them to her regularly, even though they had refused to speak to him.

They blamed her for all of their troubles. It was her fault that their son, brother, grandson, was the way he was. She must have done something to break him. That was the only logical explanation for his drastic life changes, and they needed to blame someone. They picked Luna, and for some reason she took their anger and hurt and held it close to her. She shouldn't, it was obvious that they were using her as their punching bag and she shouldn't put up with it. But Luna hadn't forgiven herself for her part in her failed marriage, so why should they?

So, she read their messages and she'd apologize. She had been doing it for months and months. The messages never got better, and they never got kinder. Her moments with her support group were the only time she felt whole again. They made her feel like she was a good person and they gave her those moments of clarity that reminded some part of her that she was worthy of their affection.

Without her friends, Luna didn't want to think of where she might have ended up.

Two years earlier

"What are you saying? Al, I don't understand. You aren't making any sense."

Luna felt like her brain was exploding and her heart was shattering. Her husband of six years was asking for a divorce.

"Lulu, you *do* know what I'm saying. It's not like you haven't considered it."

"Of course not, you're my husband. Why would I ever think that?"

Her stomach was aching and she couldn't let the words out to confirm what he was saying. She hadn't let herself think it, although plenty of people had brought it up to her. She'd tried laughing it off, and then she had become angry and indignant. How dare they suggest her marriage wasn't happy and perfect?

"Because you're smart, you're not stupid. I can't keep doing this, Lulu. I need to be honest for the both of us."

"Is there someone else?" Dear god, what if there was someone else? Another person who had stolen her man away. Someone who had convinced him to leave her? Where was the bitch? Luna would tear her a new one.

"Honey, it's not that there is someone else, it's that I need to be someone else different. I'm not saying this is new, or maybe my acceptance of it is. You know how I was raised. This is not something I even allowed myself to think about. I was even willing to live with you happily for the rest of my life.

3

I love you so much, Lulu, I'm just not *in* love with you."

Luna felt each word like a knife to the heart. *It's not you, it's me.* Except this one burned a little harder. *I love you, I'm just not in love with you.* That meant the love he was feeling for her was in his head, not his heart.

"What will people say?" She hated uttering those words, but there were so many things going through her mind that it was just the first thing that popped out. There was also explaining to everyone why they broke up. Listening to the 'I told you so's.' People looking at her like it was her fault. Which in a way, it was. She wasn't his type.

"Luna, you will say whatever you need to. Everyone is going to give their fucking opinion and I don't give a shit about them. My only concern is you. I don't want to live a life without you. I'd understand if you never wanted to see me again. I don't know if I could forgive someone for breaking my heart either. I just need something else in my life."

"Like what? Dick?"

Luna knew the words were cruel. She wanted him to hurt the same way she was. She did love him. Her heart didn't feel whole without him. How was she going to breathe if he was gone?

"Maybe? I know that I need to be true to myself. And Lulu, that is only secondary to wanting you to have everything you deserve."

"I deserve for us to be together!"

"No, you deserve to have a man who loves you heart and soul. Someone that can give you what I can't."

"Our sex life was... okay."

"Yeah, just okay. You deserve someone that will rock your world. That will make you crave them like a drug. I can't be that man for you. I never will be that."

"But I'm fine with what we have! You know sex isn't that important to me." Luna had decided a long time ago that not everyone has to have fireworks in the bedroom. Maybe she just wasn't built that way. Maybe for her it was more about the cuddling and comfort. She had tons of that from Al. In fact, he was a master cuddler. True, there wasn't a lot of spice in their relationship, but there were so many other things that made up for it. At least in Luna's mind.

"Lulu, that breaks my heart, because sex is important. It's healthy and normal to crave the person you're with. We schedule sex because we think it's been too long. That isn't love, it's obligation. I want more for you, and for me, honestly. I need to find a man that I love and that loves me. I'm gay and it's taken me way too long to be able to say that out loud. You are the first person I could even think of saying that to, because I know that you love me."

He had her there, she did love him. She also needed him so much. The air that was in her lungs had been used up and there didn't seem to be enough air left in the world for her to refill them.

She didn't know what else to say to him. So she cried. Silently. Her world was crashing down around her and there was no hope for her future to change.

~

6 months later

"Luna, I'm not saying you haven't made progress. We have been going over the same things for six months without any change in your attitude."

Luna wanted to glare at her therapist, but the woman had helped her so much she couldn't start acting like her input was new.

"Maybe my attitude isn't the one that needs changing?" Luna was sweet, normally. Her family and friends always talked about how kindhearted she was. That she didn't swear, that she barely drank. She was the first person to volunteer for something. Overall, a goody two-shoes.

"You really think that we can change everyone else? Your friends and family? We can get all of them to change their opinions. Are you still taking their calls? Reading their messages?"

"Maybe," she said, picking at an imaginary speck of lint on her pants. "Why do I have to do all the work?" That sounded shockingly petulant and childish, but it fit since she was sitting with her arms crossed and scuffing her Birkenstock foot across the floor.

"Because my job is to get you to a better place. I

want you to be happy and healthy. I'm sorry, but the rest of your family doesn't pay my rate."

"No, my ex does. How effed up is that?"

"Luna, we talked about being honest with our words. If you want to say fuck you should say it."

Luna frowned. She didn't want to say 'fuck.' It wasn't a nice word. It also didn't make her feel any better. She'd tried saying it before in the mirror, and just felt silly.

"I don't want to say the F-word. I don't want to *have* to say it. I don't want to be the type of woman that swears and turns their husband gay!"

Her therapist gave her a long look over her glasses. "You know we've also agreed to stop blaming yourself for someone else's sexual orientation. You didn't make him gay; he was gay before you met him."

"Hah! His parents don't think that. They want to know what I *did* to him. Can you believe that? Like I did some voodoo hex or something to make him want muscled beefcake over a nice pair of boobs. Did I tell you that he's seeing someone from his gym? He goes to the gym now, and tans. He TANS!"

Luna wasn't upset that Al was getting fit, or that he had decided that early onset skin cancer was worth tanning for. But he had moved on. He was dating a man named Toby who was an attorney. They met during a spin class and went out for mojitos. The rest was gay history.

"He sounds like he's happy."

"He says he is," she murmured. They still lived

together even though the divorce was final. He knew she couldn't afford the mortgage on their house alone, so he had stayed while they put it up on the market. It was going to get a good price when it sold and that should have made her happy, but it didn't.

"I'm... angry."

"Good, what about specifically. That he's happy?"

"No, I love him too much to deny him that. I'm angry that he's being so kind to me. Like I'm going to crack or have a meltdown. I haven't actually had a meltdown, not really. But he won't bring Toby over; even though I told him I didn't care."

"But you do care. You don't really want to see him being happy with someone else. You want him to be happy; you just aren't in a place to see it. He seems to know that about you."

He did know that. He had always known what she needed and when. Being in tune with her feelings was never a problem for him.

"Well, it's sweet and annoying. I'm not effing fragile!"

"Aren't you? You haven't given yourself permission to grieve yet."

"Grieve? He's not dead; he's just... into guys."

"You need to grieve the loss of the future you had planned out. The loss of the work you put into your marriage. You have suffered a loss that can't be fixed, but one that can be learned from. You had your whole life mapped out, and now you don't. You've been left in limbo while the man you loved has found someone new. What is Luna going to do to move on?"

"I don't want to grieve. It's weak and we are both still alive and I should be grateful for that."

"Yes, you can be grateful for that while still acknowledging the fact that your marriage has died."

Damn, that was brutal. Her marriage was dead, and she should be grieving. Now what?

≈

Another 6 months later

There was a feeling that couldn't be put into words. It was when a group of women came together to create a village out of the kindness of their hearts. Her friends were an army of support, love, laughter, and affection. On the fateful day when her therapist had uttered the words, 'your marriage is dead;' Luna finally started to feel the pain. She took her doctor's advice and joined a loss group. She thought it would be only for women whose spouses or family members had died, but it turned out to be so much bigger. The women circled around her and validated every thought she had been pushing away as crazy or improper. They hosted a spa night to remind her that she was beautiful and sexy, and that any man would be grateful to have her. Any straight man that was.

They had taken her to boxfit class to help her get out some pent up anger and aggression that stemmed from the feelings of betrayal that her ex had let the lie go on for so long. Then they hosted a bachelorette party to remind her that she had a future ahead of her, and being single and ready to mingle could be embraced and enjoyed.

Her squad had given her some mojo back. And as long as it was just them, she could talk the talk and walk the walk. Alone, her true feelings didn't always match up with her bravado. There were times that everything she had gone through felt like an overwhelming vise, squeezing the air out of her. Her therapist said they were panic attacks, and had given her a prescription to help combat them. It was a reminder that on the outside, she looked fixed, but on the inside, there were still some parts that were more than a little broken.

CHAPTER 2

Hair slivers, a little known side effect from cutting hair. It's just like a real wood or metal sliver, just so much harder to remove. Hairdressers got used to them, it was all part of the pain of the normal day-to-day business of using sharp scissors and trimming human hair.

Luna had stopped cutting herself a while ago. It still happened when she got distracted, or when someone called her name. But it was a rarity that she now appreciated. You could never keep that cut clean or dry. It was a lingering pain.

Lingering pain. It was funny how you could make something like that a regular part of your life. Pain that didn't fade. It would often morph or change. Sometimes you could even forget about it long enough to be distracted by something else. But it was there, hiding in the background waiting for a chance to poke its head up again.

"Luna, your two o'clock is here."

Luna looked over at her receptionist, Larissa. She was just finishing up with Mildred, one of her favorite customers. She came in once a week to get a wash and set. Luna's days usually involved a mix of men and women, cuts, trims, and lots of color. It was comforting knowing that once a week she got to wash and curl a ninety-year-old woman's hair and gossip about the people in her retirement home.

"Thanks, Rissa; tell her I'll just be a moment."

Luna could feel the sickening panic well up inside her. It wasn't that her next appointment was bad. She couldn't actually say why her skin started to feel clammy; her breathing would get short and rapid. It was a hangover from stifling her feelings for so long.

She had refused to let her mind accept her reality so she pushed it away, but her body was smarter than that and had started manifesting physical reactions to display what was going on in her head. She'd spent months on anti-anxiety medication and had been trying to wean herself off them for a while. At least while she was at work. They made her distant and slow. That wouldn't work for a busy hair salon.

Luna had opened *Salon Luna* six months earlier. It had been a lifelong dream to open her own salon. It wasn't big, just six chairs in a strip mall located in the suburbs of Denver. She had decorated it like a high-end salon but did it with a garage sale budget, with a good eye for value.

It was a huge step for Luna that was only possible

because of a year's worth of therapy and another year's worth of support from some of the best friends a woman could have.

"Miss Mildred, I declare you are looking prettier and prettier every day."

Luna turned around to see Al, Alton now, schmoozing with Miss Mildred. The only reason she had her dream salon was because of Al and Toby. It wasn't so hard a pill to swallow now. Her friends were helping her to appreciate the gifts and opportunities that had been presented to her. Maybe all the pain she had gone through was because this is where she was supposed to be.

After she and Al had sold their house, she had made enough on her share to buy a smaller house in an older part of town that she was turning into her own little haven. She had been able to put down almost half the asking price, and now she had a small mortgage that was easily manageable.

After Al and Toby had been together a while that they approached her with the idea of opening the salon. Al had gotten his cosmetology degree and was blossoming into the world of makeup, and eyelash extensions, and had goals to learn cosmetic tattooing.

Toby was determined to build a life with Alton and thought investing in their salon was better than presenting a ring.

Luna thought it was a pretty big gesture and she couldn't fault Toby for throwing all his chips in. She could see the look in Toby's eye when he was watching Alton at work. It was the look that Al had told her that she deserved from a man.

It took her ex-husband's new boyfriend to get her to understand that there is a difference between love and absolute adoration, devotion, and desire. She wanted that for herself, she just didn't know how to get it.

Taking a cleansing breath, and counting to ten, she stepped back to Miss Mildred and gave the woman's hair a final coat of extra-hold hair spray. She knew that as soon as she got home, Mildred would wrap her hair in toilet paper before she went to bed.

Miss Mildred had a rigorous beauty routine, which also involved washing her face with Ivory soap and then slathering it with Vaseline. Any normal person doing that would probably become unrecognizable between the drying and oiling of their face. However, Mildred had skin like a newborn baby and was sweet as one too.

"All done. You look fabulous, and I'll see you same time next week!"

"Oh, you always do such a nice job. You need to find a nice man to settle down with so you can get off your feet. You know, women shouldn't be on their feet all day. It wears on your joints."

"Oh Mildred, you know that this is my dream job. I wouldn't want to be doing anything else." Luna said that part with confidence. She did want to be working and running her own shop. She loved changing people's styles and making sure they walked out feeling great about themselves.

"You should find a nice boy like Alton here. He's so sweet," Mildred, said pointing at Al.

Al didn't help at all when he wiggled his eyebrows at her. Luna never saw a good reason to explain her life to strangers or customers. So she just smiled and leaned down to whisper. "He's taken."

"Oh, that's a shame. Well, there are some nice boys at my church. You should come with me some time. I'll introduce you around. There has to be at least one that will do for you."

"I'll keep that in mind."

Alton went back to his area and Luna escorted Mildred out. Her next appointment was waiting and she shook off the sweet little old woman's words and focused on being the best hairdresser she could be. She couldn't control everything in her life, but she could control her work. It had been a lifeline pulling her out of the pit of depression she'd been in for far too long.

Checking her phone, she only found two texts. One from her girlfriend Waverly and one from Alton's sister telling her she was a pathetic excuse for a woman. She shot off a message to Waverly and marked the one from Alton's sister as read.

She had other things to worry about, like her next appointment.

CHAPTER 3

"Dinner delivery!"

Luna was sweeping up around her chair from her last client. She had stayed after her regular hours to accommodate a single mom that worked full-time and couldn't get off for a haircut. Her twin boys had been racing around the salon and, luckily, not doing too much damage. Thankfully, Alton had decided to stay and help out. He spent the first half of the appointment having the little terrors build shampoo bottle pyramids.

Once her appointment left, all she wanted to do was head home to her cute little house on her cute little street, make a cup of tea, and sit on the front porch swing that she had installed. Al had offered to do it, but she had been trying to not rely on him so much. She found a pleasant handyman service that would do anything from change a lightbulb to spread mulch in your garden.

When the doorbell chimed she was surprised only at the lateness, not that the fact it was Toby carrying bags in both hands.

"I hope you brought enough to share with the whole class," Luna chimed. Her relationship with Toby was warming. He treated Alton so well that she had a hard time thinking of him as a 'man-stealing whore' like she used to. Her therapist said that wasn't constructive so she kept calling him that to herself if not in her sessions.

"Of course, I did. What kind of host do you think I am?" Toby said, winking at her and putting the bags on the counter.

"I know what kind of host you are. There were raspberries floating in our New Year's champagne. I was *so* determined to get the fruit that I tipped the glass all the way back, the berries hit my nose and splashed champagne in my eye. That shit burns, you know! So, in reality, you're a host that likes to create diabolic situations to confuse and befuddle your guests."

Toby started laughing. "You make me sound like Dr. Evil."

"Dr. Evil, with good taste," Alton corrected.

"Hey there, handsome. You hungry?"

"Depends on what you brought," Alton parried.

"Ohh, say it's Jimmy John's," Luna said gleefully. Alton's tastes had changed since he had met Toby, not that she blamed him. She and Al had been more Betty Crocker-style home cooks than anything else.

The range of their cuisine was a recipe from a book or something microwavable. However, Toby liked to eat well, and Luna got to partake in some of that good eating.

"It's not Jimmy John's, young lady. It's from Pierre's and you are going to love it!"

"Eww, French food?" Luna wasn't about to eat snails.

"Better, it's Creole. Jambalaya, shrimp etouffee, and some sweet tea to wash it down."

"That doesn't sound bad at all." Luna wasn't going to turn down real food. She had left over spaghetti at home that she had been eating for two days. It was losing its appeal.

Toby pulled out the food and arranged it on the reception counter. Luna turned off the open sign and pulled the sunshades down over the front windows. Toby handed out plates and arranged their drinks on the coffee table between the reception chairs. Toby liked things a certain way and everything took twice as long if he spent it fixing what you had done, so Luna had learned not to offer to help.

"So, Alton, did you ask her?" Toby asked after they had all started eating.

Alton looked up from his plate. "Uh, no? It's been busy today."

"Chicken shit," Toby scolded.

"Ask me what?" Luna didn't like secrets. Being out of the loop on things gave her anxiety a reason to rear up and cause chaos. Her therapist said it was a reasonable response, but that she needed to learn to trust that everyone wasn't talking behind her back or keeping things from her on purpose. The problem with that was that people were often doing both of those things.

"Toby is poking his nose into other people's business... it's shocking, I know," Alton said trying to sound annoyed but his tone came off sounding proud instead.

"Is there something wrong with the shop? We're doing well, and I know we're on track to pay back your investment on time." Luna was starting to panic; she could feel her heart starting to pound.

"Stop freaking her out, Alton. Look at her! Just breathe, Luna. It's not about the shop; everything is great. Nothing is changing with that. I was just talking to Alton saying it might be time for you to maybe... go out on a date."

Luna took a few deep breaths to calm her racing heart. Then she realized what he had said. Dating?

"Are you high? Me? Dating?"

"Yes, you. You remember dating, don't you?" Alton asked.

"No, not really." Luna really couldn't remember dating. She'd known Al since they were in high school together. They had always been together.

"Who did you date before Alton?"

"Uh, no one. Oh, wait there was that one guy I went to homecoming with. And that was only because Al had to take his cousin."

"Oh yeah! Rodney Glass, I remember him. He borrowed his dad's tux and it was a bell bottomed affair," Alton said gleefully.

"He had such horrible breath too," Luna said, cringing.

"Okay, let's look at this as an opportunity! You haven't developed any bad dating habits for us to overcome," Toby declared.

Luna couldn't help but snort. She would call some of her dating habits bad. Dating a gay man might be number one on the list of things not to do.

"Why are we even talking about dating? I'm pretty happy with my life right now. I have the shop; I have some really amazing friends. Color me happy!"

"You aren't happy, you are existing. You deserve bliss and we are going to help you find it. I already have the perfect person for you," Toby stated.

"Toby, since when do you get a vote?" Luna liked him, but this was too much.

"I get a vote because not long after I fell in love with Alton, I fell in love with *you*. You are too lovable and it's your own fault. So I want to see you happy and I've made it my mission. So I think you should go out with Ford."

"I'm sorry, Ford? Like the truck?"

"No, Ford like a friend I know from the gym," Toby said, rolling his eyes dramatically.

"Hah! And is he all muscle and no brains?"

"He works out, and has some impressive

muscles... not that I was looking," Toby confirmed pointedly at Alton.

"Pfft, like I'm the jealous sort," Alton said.

"And what do you think a muscle head guy would want with a chubby girl like me?"

"You are NOT chubby!" Both men screeched at her at the same time.

"Okay, maybe I'm not morbidly obese, but I'm not the girl I used to be. I'm thirty-three and have been eating my feelings for the last few years. No offense, Al."

"I'm sorry about that, but honestly I think you look a little better with some meat on your bones."

Since the breakup, or PA, ('post Al' she dubbed it), she had embraced the bright colorful world of high fat foods. She also appreciated that food could easily be purchased and received in the window of her car. She had put on a few pounds and it was the one thing her therapist said to worry about later. It wasn't healthy in the long run, but she was fighting bigger demons right now. With a few extra pounds here and there, her trim figure had rounded out to the point that she had developed rounded thighs which she had never known she had before.

That was when Al had stepped in again, showed her how to dress to accentuate her new figure, and she decided to roll with it. That was all good when she was the only person seeing her naked; but dating could lead to sex, and sex generally happened without clothes. She wasn't ready for any of that.

"I don't mind how I look now; it's just having to let someone else see me. That is not in my realm of coping skills right now."

"Ford is an amazing guy. He's a firefighter and is an all around great guy. Model citizen, and I think he'd love to meet you."

"Hah! Too bad for you, Toby. After he meets me he's not going to spot you at the gym anymore."

"How dare you say that about my friend! Besides, a date is just a date. It could be a nice 'get to know you.' Help you dip your foot back into the water. Why not try it? What's the worst that could happen?"

"I humiliate myself somehow and die alone in utter shame and misery?"

"Dramatic much?" Toby said with a snort.

"Really, I'd have to medicate myself into oblivion just to get to meet him. I'm just not there yet."

"You never will be until you get back in the game," Alton said softly.

"I never was *in* the game, Alton. I used you as a default," she said with a sigh. It was a recent revelation during therapy. For a while, she had thought about quitting, but even two years in, she was still not always honest with herself, but Luna also knew that she wouldn't be where she was today without her sounding board.

"No matter what, it doesn't change the fact you should meet this guy. Let us set you up." Alton was a little too excited by this idea, which made Luna worried and nervous.

"How about we all just keep going on with our lives like we always have?" Luna thought that was a much more reasonable idea. Work, sleep, and eat yummy things.

"If we let that happen you will settle into a life that revolves around settling." Alton reached over and grabbed her hand.

Luna didn't answer that because it was too close to being true. She no longer had any big aspirations for her life. Opening the salon was as big as she had thought and she had accomplished it. Why push for something else and risk failing?

CHAPTER 4

Alton and Toby hadn't pressed their agenda after dinner. They changed subjects and started talking about their upcoming vacation. They were going on a cruise for a week. Luna didn't think that going on a cruise sounded like that much fun. Not that she'd ever been on a boat before. The buffet didn't sound bad, and she heard about the all you can drink packages so you could enjoy an endless supply of adult beverages.

She'd gone home and laid down on her couch to watch her recorded shows. Her shop was open Monday through Friday with alternating Saturdays so she could get a few days off in a row. She didn't mind the work because it was something she loved, and to tell the truth, there wasn't much she did on her days off besides clean her house. It wasn't that big, so it left her with idle hands much of the time

Her phone had buzzed a few times and she

ignored it. They were probably messages from Alton's family anyway. Their reminders that she was the cause of their family's ruin and shame had trailed off over the past year. Not getting a response from her probably made the effort not as fun. But every once in a while she would get a text, voicemail, or random letter to remind her they still didn't like her. Her friends and her therapist all told her to block them, to stop giving them a voice. They were right. But she didn't. She felt it was like a penance to take their venom and soak it up. Luna didn't want to retaliate; they were going after her and not Alton. They had cut him off entirely. He didn't even know she was still in contact with them.

Maybe she should take a cruise. A vacation just for herself? Did single people take vacations on their own? She must have read about someone that did it in a magazine a while ago. Luna was sure they had called this single vacationer 'brave' just for doing what everyone else does in pairs. It was insulting. Then again, she didn't know if she was the type to go out and enjoy scenic tours and visits to museums without at least a friend to talk to about everything.

Who was she kidding? A trip with unknown variables, all by herself, wasn't who she was. She needed to know what was coming and when.

Maybe she should get a fish, something that didn't need constant attention and that she could leave for hours on end. Maybe a goldfish or two. She wouldn't want the one goldfish to get lonely.

Luna kept running over, and over in her mind the fact that Toby and Al wanted to set her up on a blind date. With a firefighter no less! The closest she was going to get to a date with a firefighter was if it was some kind of contest for charity. Then she might have a shot. Otherwise, her options were limited. She didn't even think that was so bad. Clearly, she needed to be pickier in the future. Maybe not fussy, just more cautious. Less trusting. She had forgiven Alton for keeping his secret from her. She also acknowledged that he wasn't being honest with himself, and for that, she felt bad for him.

No, Luna needed to lay low. 'Lay Low Luna' was her new street name. It would be clear to anyone that came along that she wasn't the one to step up or step out.

"A fish sounds nice."

~

Luckily, it seemed like Alton and Toby had listened to her and left her to her comfortable and predictable existence. They hadn't brought up her dating again and hadn't brought up anyone named Ford.

Ford the firefighter, it wasn't even fair. It was like watching any reality show that baited singles against each other. The men were all unattainable and the women were all catty witches. Ford probably was on one of those shows. He probably won. He was probably was handsome and tanned. Or, maybe he was one of those firefighters that could eat a dozen donuts every day and still somehow rescue people from burning buildings. She'd seen some of those firefighters. Luna heard it was from the little old ladies bringing them baked goods to thank them for checking their blood pressures, but that was just an urban legend.

Why she was thinking about this faceless firefighter was annoying, and made her feel less in control. Giving herself a mental shake, she looked into the mirror at her station and took in her appearance. It was important for her to look her best every day, especially her hair. Who would trust a hairstylist with bad hair?

Her hair changed often, because why not? Right now, it was a dark auburn with purple highlights on the underside. It had been a bold choice but Alton assured her it was the best look for her. Her makeup was on point, warm eyes, a soft shade of lipstick and just the hint of bronzer. Her outfit was usually black of some sort, it kept her look professional. Plus, she was often wearing an apron when she was dying hair, so it didn't matter what she had on underneath. Today she'd also decided to wear a pair of short-heeled mules that had a line of embroidery along the top. Her black blouse was off the shoulder and, on a whim; she'd added a choker made of velvet ribbon.

"Hot date?" Larissa asked when she got in.

"No, I just felt like not looking how I feel today. Fake it until you make it, right?"

"I get that. Let me know if it works."

"Hah, ask me around lunch time."

Lunchtime rolled around and she was still feeling pretty good. Her hair looked great, she'd managed to have enough time to grab a sandwich, and her clients had all left happy with their hair swishing.

Swishing was a sign of happiness. Any woman that left a salon running her hands through her hair, meant she was happy with her look and happy she didn't have to do it for the next few days.

Luna had just swiped on a line of lipgloss when Larissa came around the corner of her station.

"Do you have time for a men's drop-in?"

Luna checked her phone and saw she had thirty minutes before her next appointment.

"Sure, no problem."

Luna made sure her station was cleared off as Larissa left to get the customer. Grabbing a fresh cape, she looked up to see Larissa coming around the corner with a naughty but gleeful look on her face. Luna raised her eyebrow questioningly at her receptionist, and then immediately dropped it when she saw the man walking in behind her.

He was tall and wide, with soft brown hair and a huge white smile. Luna glanced away and she knew she blushed from just looking at the man. Not professional.

"Luna, this is Ford, he's here for a cut."

Ford? No, no, no. The universe would not be doing this to her. No, it wasn't the universe, it was two conniving men that were trying to play matchmaker.

Fine, she wasn't going to let them manipulate her, she was going to do her job and that would be the end of it.

"Ford, nice to meet you. Have a seat."

"Nice to meet you too, Luna." He took a seat and must have winked at Larissa, because the other woman giggled and walked away.

"Charming the receptionist will get you the best appointments you know," she said casually while swinging the cape around his shoulders.

"That was nothing. I'm saving my best moves to get the best haircut."

"I promise that you will get a good haircut, charm or not. So what are we doing today?"

Luna didn't want to touch his head but she had to. She ran her fingers through his hair assessing the length as he spoke.

"Trimmed up, need my neck shaved. I keep it short on the sides but longer on top."

"No problem, do you want me to wash it or just wet it?" Please lord let him say just wet it, she begged the universe. Massaging his scalp would probably send her in a panic attack.

This man was handsome, fit, and oh so sexy. He was not in her league at all. In fact, he was in another world of unattainable men. She was going to kick Alton and Toby's asses when she saw them.

Speaking of Alton, he was absent from the salon

today, with an excuse about an errand or something. He was being a chicken shit and hiding obviously.

"Would you mind washing it? I just gave it a rinse at the gym this morning since I was going to come here."

Of course he needed a full shampoo. Fine, she was going to be efficient and get it done.

CHAPTER 5

Ford was normally a brave man. He was a firefighter for a good reason. He never hesitated when rushing to an accident scene or when he needed to fight a fire. He just did the job and hopefully helped people in the process.

When Toby had inquired about his love life, he'd politely explained that he was into women. Which had made Toby laugh hysterically before he assured Ford that he wasn't his type.

Awkwardness aside, Toby mentioned that he thought Ford was single and whether he was in the market.

"Not in the market, exactly. I'm actually pretty tired of shopping. I just can't seem to find someone to settle down with. I'm tired of first dates that don't go well, or second and third dates where we never actually show each other our true selves and it still doesn't go anywhere. I'm tired of chasing my tail."

"Don't you mean chasing tail?"

"That's not the problem. I've had plenty of interested parties approach me, but they just see me as some hero type, or trophy lay. I want a partner. Someone to settle down with and start a family."

"So what *is* your type?" Toby appeared to be taking notes.

"I don't have a physical type exactly. I don't like super skinny. Fit is good, soft around the edges is good too. Funny is great. Willing to eat and not pick at salads when we go out. Someone that is motivated, but still needs me. It may not be fashionable, but I like to take care of someone. I need to do that. So someone that is super independent wouldn't want me around."

"What if I told you I knew a real beauty, inside and out. She managed to handle a major life blow and come out ahead. Has her own business and loves what she does. And she's also someone who really deserves a partner who can see what a treasure she is," Toby said with a sigh.

"Is she your sister? Are you trying to offload a family member?"

"No, actually, she's my partner's ex-wife."

"I'm sorry, your boyfriend's ex-wife? How does that even work?"

"It's a long story if you want to hear it."

Ford hadn't been sure that he did want to hear. This woman had to be carrying some serious baggage. Toby didn't sugarcoat any of it either. He told him how it had taken a long time for her to get over her break up and Ford didn't blame her a bit. It was one thing for your ex to fall for someone else, but for them to tell you that you were never going to be their forever was a different kind of blow. He couldn't fault her for taking the time she needed to make herself healthy again. From the sounds of it, she'd worked hard to get her head back above water.

Toby wasn't great on the descriptions, but he was looking with a different eye. Still, a good inside was better than a fantastic outside. Ford was a firm believer in inner beauty.

Now that he was sitting in Luna's chair, he saw what Toby meant about her. Luna was a beauty, the inside and out, kind of beauty. He felt his heart skip a beat the second he laid eyes on her. She blushed and that made other parts of him stand up at attention. She seemed flustered by him, which meant that Toby had mentioned him. There was recognition in her eyes when she saw him.

Then he could see she went into business mode. Ford was going to have to tame this nervous filly.

"Why don't you follow me to the wash station?"

She turned, and he was happy to follow behind her to get a view of what she was packing in the back. It was better than he had hoped. There were curves and just the slightest jiggle in her wiggle.

Taking a seat at the chair, he leaned back and tried to make eye contact. She was doing everything to not look at him. It was going to be a fun game to see if he could get her to blush again.

"So, I get the feeling that you might have heard of me before?"

"Um, someone I know mentioned someone by your name. But it could just be a coincidence."

"I don't think it's a coincidence that Toby told me all about you, he also told me that you weren't interested, so he suggested I make an appointment?"

"I'm gonna kill that effer," she mumbled.

"Don't be too mad at him. If it helps, he made you sound like someone I would really like to get to know. So he has a very high opinion of you."

"He's still a sneaky jerk. No offense, but I told him I wasn't ready to date."

"I don't think he's so concerned with you dating. It seemed to me that he just wanted you to be happy."

"Why does everyone think being with someone makes you happy? I'm happy now. What more could I ask for?"

She probably was scrubbing his scalp a little harder than necessary, but he was still enjoying it.

"More, literally more. More happiness, more fun, more sex, more excitement, just more." He wasn't sure what she wanted in life, but Ford felt that everyone should reach for the stars. Settling was a sure way to stagnate, and life was often too short for that. He saw that every day. Lives snuffed out before they even had a chance to bloom into what they could be.

So, Ford was greedy. He worked hard so he could play hard. What he really wanted was someone that could play with him.

He couldn't help but wonder if Luna would be willing.

"I worry how many people spend their lives searching for more and never getting it," Luna said.

"I think that's all about real expectations. Are you trying to get the same as someone else? Same house, same car, same vacations? Or are you searching for what you really want. Don't care about big houses? Then find the perfect small one. Don't need to drive the newest latest car? Drive something used that gets you from point A to point B. Those people are searching for someone else's dreams. Not their own."

"This salon was my dream. I have it."

"So no more dreaming for you? No more goals or wins?"

"Is that so bad?" She was running a towel over his hair.

"Not bad, just a little sad."

CHAPTER 6

Luna was sick to death of being sad. She may still have a lot of things she was still working on, but sad she was not. At least in that moment. There was nothing to be sad about.

A few years, or maybe decades from now? She might be sad that she didn't do more. Sad she didn't pick a new dream. What on earth would she dream about now? Her life goals of a happy marriage, family, and a job she didn't hate had changed. She whittled them down to being happy and having a job she felt proud of. Those were attainable because they didn't rely on anyone else. Sure, she got help with her salon, but it wasn't from someone legally, or romantically, obligated to help her.

The man under her hands was talking in a way that was not the usual banter between customer and hairstylist. He'd made the appointment to see her. He made the effort to meet her. That was unexpected and a little flattering.

She was trying her best to not look at him. Luna was treating his face like a solar eclipse. *Don't look directly at it and you won't go blind.*

"You know," she started as she sat his chair up. "Some people have been hurt and know that there can be worse things than being sad."

She put the towel around his shoulders and stood in front of him. "Let's get you cut."

Luna turned back to her station and waited for him to sit. She grabbed a comb and her scissors.

She started cutting the top and hoped that he wasn't going to start the deep talking again. She paid someone good money to help her deal with her life choices.

"Luna, would you go out with me?"

Her hands shook and she almost nipped her finger. "I don't think you want to go out with me."

"Oh, I think I do. How about I take you to the fair?"

"The fair? Is that where you normally take your dates?"

"I haven't really dated in a while, but no, in the past I'd usually stick to the dinner and movie routine. Something tells me you might be up for something with a little more fun. I'm thinking rides, funnel cakes, and some rigged carnival games."

"Oh yeah, rigged games, those are a blast. But

really, you must know something about me if you know Toby."

"I do. I know what he told me. But I'd like to get to know you myself. Give me a chance. If you don't like me; at least you'll have a little fun."

"The answer is 'yes...'" This came from the other side of her mirror and the voice was distinctly male.

"Geezus Alton, mind your own business!" Luna couldn't believe he was listening in, she hadn't even heard him come into the salon.

Alton's head poked around the mirror.

"He's hunky, he likes you, and wants to take you for funnel cake. You love funnel cakes!"

"Stop telling my secrets!"

"Oh honey, your funnel cake love is *not* a secret. Just go, and then if you don't like him you get to bitch Toby and me out later."

"Hey!" Ford said with a chuckle.

"Sorry man, it's her I'm trying to convince. Luna, go, have some fun," he pleaded.

"You know you're ganging up on me. I don't respond well to peer pressure."

"Then change your viewpoint," Ford suggested. "No pressure, your choice. You can say yes, or you can say no. Either way I'd respect your decision. But let me see if I can sweeten the deal. If I can't win you a giant stuffed animal, I'll take you out to a real dinner. And if I can swing it, I'll bring you by the fire house and let you try out the siren."

"Oh, Lulu, he knows how to flirt. That's a good deal, take it."

"You are a pushover, Al. A few flashing lights and a free meal..." Luna scoffed.

"What can I say, I'm easy," Alton said with a shrug.

"Fine! But only because I wanted to go to the fair anyway and I hate riding the Ferris wheel alone."

"Then it's a date. How about tomorrow night?"

Before she could even check her calendar, Alton piped up. "I'll get coverage for you. Go!"

"Fine, I'd be happy to accompany you to the fair. Wait, I don't even know your last name?"

"Ford Jameson," he said, reaching his hand backwards to shake hers awkwardly.

"Luna Kind," she said back. She had taken her family name back and wasn't really that upset over not being a Borlowski anymore.

"Well, Luna Kind. Looks like you better make sure I look good for my big date."

Luna gave Alton a glare and went back to finishing Ford's hair. She did do a good job, not that she could ever do anything else, and walked him to the front to pay.

"I'll pick you up here?"

"Sure, that's fine." She wasn't ready for him to invade her home haven. That was hers.

"Thanks for the cut. I'm sure the guys at the station won't make fun of me for my helmet head anymore."

"You're welcome. And I'm sorry you have such pushy friends." She was feeling more insecure now that she had agreed to go out with him. She must have been unconscious and her head had fallen forward when she agreed. It was coerced at the very least.

"I'm not," he said with a huge smile. He reached out to shake her hand and when she put her hand in his, she gasped a little at the heat between their palms. Ford gave her hand a tug and pulled her closer to him.

He kiss her cheek lightly and whispered, "See you tomorrow."

Luna watched as he walked out and stood for a moment remember how to breathe.

"Oh, he's too pretty!" Larrisa gushed.

"That is very true!" Luna murmured.

"That kiss, girl, you got a firecracker there."

"He kissed you? Already!?" Alton said way too loudly. He had been snooping in the back and had somehow missed the kiss.

"It was on the cheek, settle down," Luna said turning on him.

"Lulu, don't get mad. I love you, and I just didn't want you to pass up a chance at some fun, and maybe something more than fun."

"You are putting a lot of hopes into a guy that Toby knows from the gym. He could be a serial killer. Toby would ignore that fact just because he can do squats or bench lift some stupid amount of weight."

"Honey, he's a lawyer, he's not stupid," Alton said.

"Being a lawyer makes him smart about law, not life. This could be terrible. He may realize I'm not his type and abandon me in the tunnel of love or something. Gawd, my therapist would be able to afford a vacation house if that happened."

"First, they don't have tunnels of love anymore. He'd be more likely to leave you while you are waiting in some stupid bathroom line. That's what I would do."

"Good to know," Luna said walking by him and slapping at his arm.

She wasn't really mad at him; it was one of the major flaws of their relationship. She had a very hard time being angry with him because she always knew that his intentions were pure.

Still, now she had a date to look forward to. A date with a hunky man that smiled at her as though she might just be something he liked.

At least the fair would have a lot of distractions. Bright lights and games could help if they couldn't find anything to talk about.

CHAPTER 7

"You guys, I need advice."

Luna had gotten home and called for reinforcements. She Skyped with her girls that were online. Her friends Waverly, Elena, and Cambry were all online staring at her with various degrees of shock on their faces.

"Uh, advice like, jump his bones?" Cambry offered. She was happily in love, and was all for everyone going full throttle towards potential happiness.

"You shouldn't get a vote. You're getting it regular," Elena said with a snarky tone.

"Jealous much?"

"Hells yes, we are jealous. Some of us are still relying on mechanical interventions," Waverly overshared.

"I feel like I'm on a soap opera every day. 'My gay ex-husband's new boyfriend set me up with his gym buddy.' What's next? A convenient coma or amnesia?"

"Oh, that does sound like a good show," Elena said while munching on popcorn. Apparently, the best show on tonight was 'Luna's Love Life.'

"He's so out of my league, girls. He's tall, like really tall... and muscles, he had muscles everywhere. I swear he had muscles in his hair."

"I think you are suffering from a serious set of pity goggles," Waverly suggested.

"Pity goggles? Seriously?"

"You can't see yourself like others do," Cambry agreed. "You are beautiful, Luna. This man came in, saw you with his own eyes and still asked you out. Do you think he was blind?"

"Maybe he couldn't think of a way to get out of the obligation? I mean I knew why he was showing up, and if he didn't ask me out after he saw me, which would have been worse, Toby would have sued him for breach of promise or something."

"Yeah, I don't think that's possible, sweetie," Elena said around a mouthful of food.

"What man would go out with a woman whose husband left her because he's gay? What if he thinks that I knew and still married him because I didn't think that I had any other options? What if he thinks that Al was so repulsed by me that I turned him gay, OR what if he thinks that I was so bad in bed that Al figured he'd give men a try?"

Waverly made a growling noise before saying,

"Honey, I say this with love and affection. Stop being a fucking idiot. One, he was always gay. You know that's how it works. If you are bad in bed, a straight guy will cheat on you with another woman. And two, there is no way you repulsed anyone. You are all woman, complete with curves and sexy hair, you might not realize it, but you strut when you walk. These are all very appealing things to a smart man. Ford sounds like a smart man. So shut up, get off the pity pot and take some of that positive reinforcement that years of talking about yourself in therapy should have bought you, and have fun."

"Yeah, what she said," Elena said. "Stop being a pussy."

"Dude, don't call her a pussy. Pussies are nice. We all have one and shouldn't talk down about it. Tell her to stop being a testicle. Those are delicate and overly protected. Yeah, stop being a big ball, Luna." Cambry obviously thought that she was being incredibly clever.

"I can never tell if I hate you guys or love you guys."

"Oh, you know," Waverly said with a wink.

"Fine, I fucking love you guys. Did you hear me? I said fuck. I've been practicing."

"It still freaks me out a little," Cambry admitted. "It's like a nun swearing."

"Oh, and don't wear your ugly undies because you think you won't get laid. Because you'll be embarrassed, and he won't give a shit when he's ripping them off you," Elena said wisely.

"Ugly undies, the dreaded double U. Never a good idea. Dress yourself from the inside out in things that make you feel confident. Go on the Tilt-a-Whirl, you get to touch by centrifugal force, it's sexy."

"I'll squish him!"

Waverly shook her head. "Honey, he'll love it."

"Fine, what do I wear?"

The girls went over clothing choices and decided on something that would hold up well at a fair and the massive amount of dirt that went with it and gave her a few last minute pointers.

Only Luna's friends could Skype for two hours and make the time fly by.

The next morning she packed a bag with the outfit they had chosen, because there was no way she was wearing clothes that smelled like burnt hair and product on a date.

During the day, Luna tried to keep her focus, chatting with her clients, not looking off into the distance worrying about her date. At the last minute, she had packed her meds in the bottom of the bag with her clothes. It had been weeks since she had taken them, but just having the bottle was a kind of security blanket.

Whenever she wanted to reach for them, she took a deep breath and counted very slowly to ten. Then she reassessed whether she needed to take them or if could she breathe and count again. She spent a long time breathing and counting these days. Every pill she didn't take was a small victory. Luna understood that for some people, having them was the only way to get through a day. For her, it was about getting her old self back, so she was using them as a tool more than anything.

Luna thought about the pills at the bottom of the bag again. She didn't want to be fuzzy for her date, and the meds made her feel calmly distant. This was her first date in years and she wanted to be fully involved so she wouldn't make a jackass of herself.

Then again, they were going to a fair and that was fraught with potential hazards.

"How are you wearing your hair?" Alton had snuck up behind her and was moving her hair around as she had zoned out at her station after her last client.

"Um, down?"

"Did you not see that poor girl that got her hair stuck in a carnival ride recently? No ma'am, you are not ending up on the news. I'm thinking high double pony, teased."

"You were thinking about how I should wear my hair on my date? My ex-husband shouldn't have an opinion on that topic."

"Your bestest friend in the whole wide world has an opinion. And tell me I'm wrong."

It was true, he was her best friend. They had been together too long to deny their connection, or their place in each other's lives.

"Fine, ponytail. But I need a poof on top. Something for height."

"What are you wearing?"

"Clothes."

"Har-har, seriously."

"Capri jeans, the cut off ones rolled up. My *Rolling Stones* t-shirt and my wedge high tops to make me taller, but are still comfy."

"No jacket? You might need a jacket."

"Gee, thanks, dad. I have my jean jacket, the crop one. Anything else?"

"No, I think that will do. Let me know when you want makeup and we'll get you dolled up."

"Nothing over the top. I'm going to the fair, not performing on the main stage at the fair."

"Fine, no glitter. You spoil all my fun," he said turning in a fake huff.

Luna wasn't about to show up looking like a peacock. She was nervous enough and had already skipped her lunch because she was feeling queasy.

She had two more appointments for the day, and then she had scheduled an hour and half to get ready. That would be time to dress, do her hair and makeup and then have a major freak out before he arrived.

CHAPTER 8

Ford was sitting in his car watching the clock on the dash. He didn't want to be too early and didn't want to be late. He had told some of his buddies at the station about his date and they gave him an equal amount of ribbing and encouragement.

The men and women at the firehouse were like family. Not that Ford's large family wasn't constantly involved in his life, but he was lucky in that he had multiple families to draw strength and support from. The only thing he was missing was a partner. He wanted someone to come home to. He worked odd hours and knowing that there was someone to check in with, discuss dinner with, and all the other minutia of daily life sounded infinitely comforting.

His level of concern about Luna's history had dissolved as soon as he saw her. Now he felt like he was on a mission. There were twenty stories ahead of him and he was carrying a hundred pounds of gear.

The good thing was that he knew what kind of fortitude he had, and took the challenges head on. There was also a part of him that wanted to take care of this broken bird. For all of her outward glamour and confidence, her feathers had been damaged, and she was afraid to fly again. Ford was going to make sure that she knew that even if it wasn't because of him, although he planned to exert every effort to make sure it was because of him, that she was going to come out okay in the end.

Grabbing the vase of flowers from the passenger seat, he stepped out into the sunshine.

The moment he opened the door of the salon, he was greeted with a huge smile from the receptionist. Larissa, he thought her name was. She was practically bouncing in her seat, she must have been expecting him.

"I'll tell her you're here. Oh, you brought flowers! You, handsome devil, you."

He gave her a smile and a wink that made the woman giggle. Ford didn't flirt intentionally, he just liked women and he loved to make them smile or laugh. It was like watching a sunrise or seeing an amazing rainbow. Women were nature's gift to men that surely didn't deserve them.

Alton came around the corner and Ford held out his hand. "Alton."

"Ford. If I didn't like you so much I'd give you the 'hurt her and I'll kill you speech.'"

"I appreciate that, but I'd understand if you did.

She seems pretty amazing. I thought she might have liked me a little yesterday."

"Well, she liked the look of you, that's for sure. She only blushes like that when she thinks someone's good-looking." Alton dropped his voice. "I shouldn't interfere, but I love her to death and I just want her to be happy. If she's not your type, just let her down easy. Luna's in a good place and I don't want to have to start over. I hurt her a lot and I take responsibility for that. For her sake, I'm now her guardian angel against the big bad world."

Ford could respect this man that was in a very difficult position. "I have no intention of hurting her. I like her. I hope that I can get to know her better. I'm looking for something more than a casual date."

"I'm glad to hear that. I love her with all my heart, but not the way she deserves. I want her to be happy. She doesn't see that she isn't happy, it's one of her few faults. I'm not saying she's not strong. She is, she just doesn't think that she's the type of woman any man would want. That's most definitely, partly, but still mostly my fault. Everyone else can tell her all day long that she's come through a lot. It doesn't mean she's going to believe any of it," Alton said.

"I appreciate the tips. I think I'm going to just have a good time tonight and I'll make sure that Luna has fun."

"Do that, she could use some fun."

Ford shook his hand again and then looked up to see Luna coming around the corner. She looked amazing. Her outfit was hugging her curves and he could finally see what her apron had been hiding. She was dressed casual, but still completely put together. It was something Ford loved about women. They could act as though they had thrown something on, but he knew that everything had been chosen with care. The wedges she was wearing brought her up almost to his shoulder, but she still had to tilt her head back to look at him. There was a nervous smile on her face and he thought it made her look exquisite.

"Luna," he said and watched the blush spread over her cheeks.

"Hey," she said, tucking a stray strand of hair behind her ear even though it was already perfectly in place.

"Ready to have some fun?"

"I am. Alton wasn't giving you some speech about taking me out and not hurting my feelings or anything."

"No, he was just telling me that he liked my jeans."

"That's believable, but I don't believe you."

Alton walked past her and squeezed her arm. "Have fun."

"Thanks, I will." She sounded confident but there was an air of unease about her.

Ford could handle unease, that meant she was nervous but still had the guts to show up. That was a start.

"You look amazing," he said, eyeing her up and down.

"Thanks, I wasn't sure what to wear."

"Well, I have a feeling we are going to smell like sugar and carnies later."

"Oh, pleasant. Just so you know, I don't do rides that flip upside down. It's unnatural and messes with my hair."

"Understood. Besides I can think of a lot better ways to mess up your hair."

With that, he grabbed her hand and waved to the receptionist. He knew that she was behind him with her mouth open in shock and he decided he liked that look on her too.

Maybe if he kept her a little off guard she wouldn't get so hung up on what was in her head and could relax a little.

"Mind if I drive?"

"No, that's fine. You're a good driver aren't you?"

"No tickets and I've been known to drive the fire truck around for fun."

"Is that true?"

"No, not really. There are so many jobs at the fire-house that very few people can do everything. I do know how to use the fire truck. There are lots of fun levers and buttons."

"Oh, levers and buttons. I can see why you got into the business," she joked.

"Actually, I love the adrenaline. I was eighteen when I started volunteering. I thought it would be all action. Fires and car accidents. Turns out, we have a lot of down time and that's a good thing. Down time means no one is dying and property isn't being destroyed. I started working out so I could do my job better and kill some time."

Ford helped Luna inside the car and shut the door behind her. As he walked to the driver's side, he glanced through the front windshield and saw a very nervous looking Luna watching him. He smiled at her and watched her blush and drop her gaze. He made it around to the driver's side and got in.

"Did you always want to be a firefighter?"

Clearly, she wanted to fill the space with conversation, that's what you did on first dates as to avoid any awkward lulls. Ford was fine with that, he wanted her to know all about him, and he really wanted to get to know her better.

"I did. My dad and uncle were firefighters and it was what I was surrounded by. You could say that it's in my blood."

"I think it's very brave. I can't imagine running into a burning building."

"I've only had a few opportunities to do that. We spend a lot of time responding to road accidents. And then the rest of the time responding to non-emergencies."

They had started to drive and he was taking in her body language. She was sitting with her knees pressed together and her hands in her lap.

"Non-emergencies?"

"Frequent fliers and situations that really don't need us. It's a lot of standing around and waiting. It's the less glamorous part of our job."

"Compared to what I do it sounds pretty glamorous."

"I don't know; you make people feel good. I bet people look forward to seeing you. They use that time to get away from their lives and you make sure they look amazing when they leave. I deal with bodily fluids and sometimes death. Your job is important. I can't imagine anyone wants to see me coming."

Luna held back the hysterical giggle that popped up. She was sure some of his calls were just so he and his potentially hot coworkers might show up. "I'll let you keep thinking that."

"Hey, we all have our parts to play. I wouldn't begrudge the person that makes my food or that mows the lawns in intersections. Everybody has a role."

"So, enough about how vital my job is. Do you have any siblings?"

"I do. I have three brothers and two sisters."

"Six children?" she said in horror.

"Yes and I'm the middle child. Well, me and my sister, we share the title. Big Irish family. Loud, lots of food, and lots of meddling."

"A set of twins too! Sounds nice. I just have my sister and my dad. My mom passed away when I was thirteen. I had to step up for my little sister. My dad and I were a team."

"Sorry about your mom. That's a lot of responsibility for a young girl."

"It was, but you don't always get to choose your life. It sort of happens to you."

Ford didn't believe that at all, but it said a lot about how Luna viewed the world.

"Maybe it does. Sometimes though, it's all good that happens."

CHAPTER 9

Luna was having that surreal feeling as though she was viewing the world from the outside. She was riding in Ford's car and he was telling her about his life. She told him about her mom without thinking. Normally this was something she kept to herself. People always got that sad uncomfortable look in their eyes when they imagined a young teen girl losing her mother and having to look after for her younger sibling.

It wasn't that bad. Her sister, Astrid, was two years younger so they were both old enough to manage themselves for the most part. Her dad kept their world as simple as he could. He worked and managed to do fun things with them when he was off. Her childhood wasn't always bad. They were like any other family, but her mom's illness had been quick and her death had left them shocked.

But they recovered. Then she met Al. Her life was

moving on then. She got married and they had made a life together.

But that was all gone now, and she didn't have much at all.

Now her simple world was looking like there were options in the future. Paths her road could take, and she didn't know which way to turn. One might have a hunky firefighter option. The other, well it was unknown, and oddly enough, she wasn't in the mood for the unknown.

"I bet your family is really proud of you," she said. Talking about his family was a much safer topic. Less chance of her getting nervous.

"They are. My parents are proud of all their children. I've got siblings that are police officers, stay-at-home parents, construction workers, managers. They told us we could be anything we wanted as long as we were happy."

"Must be nice. I bet holidays are fun."

"They are chaotic. I have three nephews and five nieces. It's loud, but it's wonderful."

Luna couldn't imagine what it was like to have such a noisy house. Her father's home was sedate. There weren't big parties after her mom was gone. Quiet birthdays, simple Christmases. It was all very tolerable.

"I bet. Although I have to say, Toby and Alton threw a huge party last year. It was a little more than I was used to."

"How so?"

"Everything was very shiny. And it all matched. Like really matched. And Christmas dinner was catered. It was very nice, but a little too formal for my liking, but it was fun to do something different."

They chatted easily as they drove, and then parked in a large lot that flanked the fair grounds. As they got out of the car there was a warm breeze filled with sugar and the smell of farm animals.

"So what should we do first? Animals? Rides? Games?"

"Oh, let's see if they have any baby animals!"

Ford chuckled. "Like the animals do you?"

"I do. Especially the baby pigs and ducklings. I was thinking of getting a fish. Something I won't feel guilty about leaving at home."

"I'll see if I can win you a goldfish or two."

"Those are really expensive fish. You know buying them is cheaper than what you spend on those games. You know they're rigged, you've said it yourself!"

"It's still more fun to win them."

"Fine, but let's do it last so we aren't walking around all night with little fish suffocating in a bag."

"I know CPR so we'll be okay."

He reached for her hand and she let hers slip into his. It was a little forward for a first date. She knew that much, but it felt comforting and her mind tripped into a strange mode that she'd never felt before. It was safe and protected. Just Ford's presence beside her felt like a shield.

There wasn't a time she could think back to that

felt this way. Ford was weaving through crowds of people, blocking her against those that might be in the way. She knew that if she stayed beside him that, she was in a safe space. The thought almost made her laugh aloud. Maybe she was just desperately searching for something that made her think this way. Luna was anxious and nervous generally, but being afraid was a different emotion entirely. While she was inside the 'Ford bubble,' there was no fear. He was big and strong and was used to facing terrible things and coming out the other side. He was a proverbial knight in shining armor.

"You know your way through a crowd."

Ford turned back to her and grinned. "I've spent a lot of time around crowds of people. I don't like lingering. Do you mind?"

"Not at all, forge ahead!"

Ford got them to the ticket booth in record time. He also paid for their admission even when she tried to protest.

"My date, I pay."

"So if I ask you out, will I get to pay?"

He pretended to ponder that for a moment. "Nope."

"Hey, that's not fair. I can pay for things too, you know."

"I know you can, but around me, you won't."

"That's ridiculously archaic!"

"I know. I'm such a caveman. It's who I am. Besides, you don't understand that if my mom, or any of the guys at the station, found out that I let a woman pay for me, they would give me a ration of shit that may last years."

"It's the twenty-first century, aren't we beyond that?"

"Intellectually yes, in my heart, no. I can't help it, it's in my nature to provide. I get a sense of pride and accomplishment in taking care of others. You wouldn't want me to stop being myself would you?"

"Well, no. Way to make me sound like a monster why don't you."

"Here's the thing, I know you can pay. So, allowing me to pay gives me something. It's like a gift from you to me. So, thank you."

"Why do I get the feeling I've just been bamboozled?"

"Don't worry, I'll get you some sugar and it'll wear off."

Ford did get her some sugar. A huge cone of cotton candy that was three different colors.

"I think this much sugar right off the bat might not be a great idea."

"It will give us energy. I'm thinking rides first, then food again, and then games, then more food."

"Got it all planned out, do you?"

"I used to be a Boy Scout, I'm always prepared."

They shared the giant cotton candy and when Ford didn't think she was taking enough he started feeding her pieces.

It was awkward because no matter how hard she

tried to avoid the contact, his fingers kept touching her lips. Luna knew her face was probably glowing red with embarrassment.

"You are so pretty when you blush."

She couldn't imagine that being true. "Tomato red is the new 'hot' color?"

"On you it makes me think of other places and times you might be red and flushed. It's a nice picture for me."

Did he just say what she thought he said? No, that wasn't standard flirting and might be pushing the bounds of decency.

"Uh..."

Ford leaned down to her ear to say quietly, "In case you weren't sure, I'm thinking of what you would look like under me, naked and sweating. It's a pretty picture."

Luna almost choked on her cotton candy. Sex. With him. Dear lord, she'd never survive. She was wearing her jean jacket because while she was in the salon, she had realized that every time she thought about him her nipples got hard. Her jacket was covering up some of the evidence that she was responding to his words. Maybe it had been too long, but he painted a picture in her head that was hot and didn't sound bad at all.

These were some crazy new emotions she was dealing with. Life with Al had not been a steaming bed of sexual tension. It was a comfortable blanket of affection.

Ford made her jittery and tense. Her body was screaming out for something that she wasn't sure she was ready to embark on.

"Ford..."

"No pressure, but just in case you were thinking that I wasn't interested in you in that way. Whatever might have been in that pretty little head of yours telling you this isn't a real date. You're wrong. This is a real date because I like you and want you to like me too."

"I'm not good at this."

"Good at what? Having fun?"

"Dating! I haven't really dated and I feel like I might do something wrong."

Ford grabbed the last of the candy and threw it in a nearby trashcan. He turned back to her and sucked his thumb into his mouth to wet a spot of stickiness left. That thumb left his mouth and moved over her bottom lip, she could feel the wetness over her trembling mouth.

"Lick it."

She did, it was automatic that her tongue move over the cool dampness he'd left. When she did, her brain realized what she had done.

Luna tried to step back and Ford's hands came up to her face.

"You've already had a taste; there shouldn't be anything uncomfortable between us now."

Ford brought his mouth to hers and kissed her.

Luna was half frozen half a trembling mess. She

gasped at how warm and sweet his mouth was as he swept his tongue into her mouth.

He tasted like spun sugar and man. It was too much for her and she melted against him. She felt strong arms circle her and pull her tight against him. He was supporting her whole body as he captured her mouth.

Luna should have cared that they were making out in front of a thousand of strangers, but her mind was preoccupied with cataloging everything about Ford that was different from the handful of kisses she'd received in her life. He didn't kiss like the those junior high boys behind the bleachers. And he certainly didn't kiss like Alton with his sweet, gentle, bordering on 'friends only' type affection.

His strength showed in his kiss. He took charge, taking her mouth while urging her to respond. She did, hesitantly. Not sure what exactly she was supposed to do.

Ford leaned back and his eyes were glistening with something that made Luna shiver. His hand came up between them and she thought he would touch her lips again. Instead, his thumb came up and rubbed her forehead between her eyes.

"Busy in here," he said.

He wasn't wrong. Her mind was firing on too many topics.

"Sorry, I just…"

"It's okay. I'll get it to turn off."

"Hah, good luck. Years of therapy and medication haven't made that happen."

"Then it's time to try something new."

Ford kissed her again and this time she had a little less static in her mind as her body and mouth remembered what to do.

This kiss lasted a little longer and ended when Ford's hands cupped her bottom and pulled her up against the hardness between them.

It was a bit of a shock that she hadn't thought about what state he might be putting himself in making out with her in public.

She heard him make a growling noise as he broke their kiss. His head dropped down to hers. "I better stop. I'm all for public displays of affection, but my brain was just trying to convince me to find somewhere to get a better taste of you."

"Ford!"

"Just being honest, babe. I think we better find a way to distract ourselves. What do you say?"

"Good idea," she said looking around to see who might have been watching them. She didn't make any eye contact, but then again, staring would have been rude too.

Luna wasn't sure if she was going to be able to spend the rest of the evening not replaying those kisses over and over in her head. She wanted to message her friends and tell them she had already been kissed. They would probably be proud of her and tell her to lock him in a basement and keep him forever. Then again, their advice wasn't always practical.

They walked around looking at different booths that were selling everything from food to souvenir pictures. It gave her an idea.

"Hey, why don't we take a selfie and send it to Toby and Alton to prove we actually went on our date?"

"Sure, just send it to me too. I will need proof next time the guys at the firehouse give me shit for being a monk."

Luna pulled out her phone and opened the camera. She quickly realized it would be a very unflattering picture from her angle. Handing him the phone she instructed, "Okay, now arm up high, angle it down so we are looking up and don't have double chins."

"Babe, we don't have double chins."

"Speak for yourself. And take a couple just in case."

"Just in case of what?"

"We have to pick the best one. Filters can only do so much, you know."

Ford took the pictures then handed her back her phone. She sent the picture off to Alton, Toby, and Ford with a message of having fun at the fair. Her phone buzzed back within thirty seconds with a message.

"Alton said to remember to wash our hands after touching the animals. That's helpful," she laughed.

Ford laughed and took her hand and started walking again. Luna managed to copy the picture over and send it to her girls with no explanation. She didn't want to be rude, so she tucked her phone into her jean pocket and had to keep her giggles to herself as her phone practically blew up. The vibrations from the messages were making her legs tingle.

They must approve.

CHAPTER 10

Ford kept to his plan. His goal was to keep them so busy that he wouldn't try to drag her back to his condo and spend the next twelve hours making love to her. That one kiss had set into motion a series of thoughts in his head that he couldn't control.

Well, to be honest he could control them, but he didn't want to. They were too good. That kiss stated potential. It was hot, and she had responded so timidly at first, and then he got a moment or two that told him that Luna was more than meets the eye. She had passion, it was just untapped, and there was nothing he liked more than a challenge.

Luna was triggering all of his instinctual buttons. He wanted to protect her, provide for her, and fuck her six ways to Sunday. These were thoughts he'd shared with her outright but he didn't go into detail. They were his own feelings and he was man enough to admit it when he saw something that he liked. He wanted Luna. He could almost say that he needed her. It wasn't like him to rely on someone else, but Luna could be someone he could see in his future.

Not wanting her to have time to overthink, he kept her moving. He bought them wristbands that let them go on any ride. They rode the roller coaster and his heart skipped a little not from the excitement of the ride, but from the sheer joy on Luna's face. Her laughter was contagious and it looked like she was having a great time.

In between rides, he took the opportunity to kiss her again. Not like their first or their second kiss, just short hot kisses that kept her cheeks flushed and her eyes shining. Luna Kind was wiggling her way into his heart and he wasn't prepared for the depth of that feeling. Sure, she was sexy, but there was something else about her.

"Time for food?"

"After all that sugar we ate? That was probably a daily total for calories in one serving."

"Yeah, I'm not buying it. I'm starving, so you must be hungry too. And I'm thinking we can get a sample of a few things and see what we like?"

"So, overeat and then more rides? That's a recipe for disaster."

"Eat, games, then more rides. Need to let everything settle a bit. I'd hate to embarrass myself by throwing up in front of you."

"Oh gawd, I think I'd die of embarrassment."

"If I vomited?"

"Yes, because if you do, I will, and then it will be a whole thing."

"Wow, you wouldn't last long in my job. Like I said, it can get messy."

Ford walked towards a long row of food stands and the overwhelming aroma of so many foods mixing should have been repulsive. Instead, it made his stomach growl and Luna looked almost giddy.

He stopped at a stand that was making smothered fries. He ordered some, then went over to a stand that had chicken fried rice served in a pineapple. He had his eye on some piroshkies and grilled corn. Grabbing those, they made their way to a picnic table under a tent with their haul.

"Here you get us organized and I'll grab drinks. Soda or lemonade?"

"Ohh, lemonade, please."

Ford like the twinkle in her eye. She was having fun and that made him incredibly happy.

Coming back with their drinks he saw she had organized the table in some fashion and was waiting for him.

"You could have started without me."

"Cute that you would think I would. Besides I had to lay them out by carb content and junk food level."

"What did you come up with?"

"Unfortunately, everything you got is all carbs and fat."

"Nothing unfortunate about it. This is all necessary fair food. Plus, I got enough that we can eat slowly and chat."

"I shouldn't eat all of this. It's so bad for you."

"It's not great for you, but I'm sure we'll figure out a way to work it off."

"Ford! Really?"

"Absolutely really. What do we start with first?"

"Fries, let's start easy."

Ford dug into the fries and they laughed, as it was impossible to pick them up. He found them some forks to make consumption easier. She told him some funny stories from her work. About the first time she turned someone's hair green when she was just starting out. He nodded and added in when he needed to. Mostly he was just watching her. She was so bright and alive, and she probably didn't see that in herself.

He watched her hesitate a few times, her eyes sliding over to something she wanted to eat and he could see her pull back. Stupid media convincing woman to not eat. It pissed him off. So what if she had some weight on her? She was all woman and soft and curvy was what he wanted to hold at night. If other men liked skinny, good for them. That wasn't what he wanted.

When her eyes traveled to a container on the table, he would just scoop up whatever it was and offer it to her. She always took it. She would chew, a little look of pleasure would hit her eyes, and it made Ford greedy for more of those looks.

"I think I'm full. Seriously, I ate too much," she said finally.

"I have to agree with you there. I shouldn't have shoved in that last piroshky. I love those things. We need to walk and digest. May I escort you through the vendor building? You might find a new wonder mop that you desperately need. Or some handmade candles?"

She gave a laugh. "Just don't let me leave with a flag pole. That's happened before."

"Seriously, a flag pole?"

"Yes, I needed one for my new house and it was collapsible. It was also huge and expensive."

"Okay, I'll help you restrain yourself from giant flagpoles."

Ford dumped their trash and walked slowly towards the large building that held the vendors. It was warm out and the air-conditioning would feel good. He took her hand and she slid in next to him as if they had done it a million times.

CHAPTER 11

Luna wasn't nervous anymore. She wasn't quite sure when that feeling of inner dread had slipped away. Maybe it was on the Tilt-a-Whirl or the Scrambler where they were laughing so hard because Ford kept squishing her when the car whipped to the outside. Being with him was getting easier. It was almost comfortable, and she was surprised by it.

They walked into the building that was packed with people, vendors, crying children and the smell of burnt popcorn. Luna spied the ladies' room.

"Do you mind if I stop for a minute?"

"Sure, take your time. I'll be over here looking at tin beer signs. Because you can never have enough of those."

"I'm sure."

Luna made quick work in the bathroom and then pulled out her phone. Ignoring the message from Alton's grandmother that consisted of sad face emoticons and misspelled words, she sent a group text to her friends.

Luna: He kissed me!
Cambry: Shut up!
Waverly: Oh, he's good!
Luna: I ate tons of junk food in front of him. He made me!
Waverly: Made you? Girl no man has to force me to eat junk.
Elena: What did I miss?
Elena: Kissed? Junk Food? Is this a dream date?
Paisley: He kissed you at the fair? Does he have a fetish?
Cambry: I know he's hunky and he feeds you. I'm loving this. Ignore Paisley.
Luna: He keeps hinting at other things. Like other things...
Cambry: He's moving fast. Gotta love that.
Luna: Not loving that. What am I supposed to do?
Elena: Where are you now?
Luna: Bathroom.
Waverly: Get back out there and have fun. Give yourself permission to do what feels right. It's not hard. You make the choice and you are in control.
Luna: You think?
Cambry: He sounds nice, and your ex-husbands boyfriend approves of him so he must be okay.
Luna: Har-har you're a riot.
Luna: Fine, but if I send a 911 later, you need to call Alton for a rescue op.
Waverly: I have a feeling we won't be hearing from you for a while.

Luna: Thanks for that.
Elena: Take pictures
Luna: Sick bitch.
Elena: Proud of it.
Gianna: Shit, I came in late. Kiss him back, then find a dark corner and check out his corn dog.
Adalyn: Oh my god I can't believe you just said that.
Dawn: Ignore them and have a good time!

Luna went back out to find Ford looking at a book of crocheted baby hats.

"Something you need to tell me?" she quipped.

"I have a big family, someone is always announcing they're pregnant. I've started buying gifts and storing them in the closet. Surprise baby shower? Boom, I've got it covered. I usually buy them something that they want, something I like, and then follow up with the usual firefighter baby gear. They are my nieces and nephews so I figure they can represent their uncle."

"I'm guessing they are all very well loved."

"Spoiled and smothered. We don't know any other way. I'm jealous of my siblings. They have their own families and I hope that I can fit one into my lifestyle."

"Fit it in?"

"I work sometimes twenty-four on twenty-four off. I'll do four days on then four days off. I'll sleep at the station. It just depends. I would hate to miss anything. You know they grow up so fast. What if I miss a first step or a first word? How do you get those moments back?"

"I'm sure that your partner would record them. Or make sure you're included. Your kids would know that their dad does a really important job and that the sacrifices are worth it. Military kids know that, cop kids, and I'm sure firefighter kids too. My dad worked a lot because he had to. I didn't blame him. I knew that he had work to do."

"I guess kids are more understanding than adults sometimes."

"Does someone important to you not like your job?"

"No, it's just that I've dated in the past and it was tough not being available all the time. I'd say I'd call and then get on a job and not be able to get back to them. It made them feel like they weren't important, which wasn't the case at all. I just had to focus on my work first."

"I understand that. I mean you have to not let distractions in while you work. Who wouldn't understand that?"

"A lot of people actually. I'm not saying it's bad, I'm just saying that they might need someone with a nine to five."

"I spend a lot of time at the salon. I often work late hours."

"Sounds like we both understand busy schedules. That's nice, yeah?"

"What are you getting at?"

"Nothing, I'm just saying that you wouldn't be surprised by my schedule and I wouldn't be surprised by yours."

"Do we need to be okay with each other's schedules?"

"Luna, I'm thinking that it's going to be very important soon. Because I've had a really nice time. I hope our evening continues. And even though I work tomorrow for twenty-four, I'd like to see you the next day. Maybe an early breakfast?"

"So, you want a second date?"

"I'll be honest I don't want this date to end. If I didn't have to work I'd take you home and keep you there until I had to give you back to work."

Luna wasn't sure what to say to that. Who heard of a first date that lasted for days?

"I'm probably going to regret this, but what would we do for a little over a day?"

"I'd start with finishing out tonight by winning you those goldfish. Then we'd have to do a late night trip to buy them a home. Which I would kindly offer to help you set up at my house first. Maybe then, I'd convince you to sit on the couch with me. Offer you a glass of wine if you want. I'd try to get you to kiss me again. Then if you were willing I'd spend the better part of the night getting to know you, hopefully naked."

"Ford, are you for real?"

"Absolutely. You don't have to guess with me, Luna. If you want to know how I'm feeling just ask."

Luna thought that was dangerous and not something she'd ever let anyone do to her. Even if she was going to try and tell the truth, she'd stutter her way through it and come out looking deceitful.

"Do you like me?"

The words tumbled out as if someone else was making her ask. Shit! What if he said no? But why would he? He just made her a proposition that wasn't at all subtle.

"Of course. I like you a lot. I think you're sexy as hell. You're beautiful and I've had fun tonight. Why wouldn't I like you?"

Luna shrugged. "I have baggage. I get anxiety. I see my therapist regularly and she's prescribed me medication for it. I'm not perfect."

"Do you really think anyone is perfect? I can tell you right now that they aren't. I've met so many people in my job, from the poorest of the poor to the richest of the rich. Nothing excludes anyone from having issues. We all do the best we can with the life we are given. I can only say from the brief time I've spent with you, and what Toby told me, that you are a fighter. I like that. Strong people are attractive."

"Me? Strong? I have never used that word in describing myself. I would pick something opposite. I hate that I haven't always been able to manage on my own. I wish I could have handled things without help."

"Why?"

"Because then that would make me a strong capable person."

Ford moved closer to her and since they were in a very public place with people milling around them, he leaned down so only she could hear him.

"You are strong, capable, and brave. You came out with me even though you were scared to do so. I know you don't know me, but I'll let you know something for the future. I don't like anyone close to me to talk badly about themselves. You are now close to me. I don't care if you think these things in your head, but as someone that matters to me, I can't let you be mean to yourself. I'll make sure to remind you regularly that you are amazing and we will work to keep those negative thoughts away, yeah?"

Luna had always spoken badly about herself. Her squad had helped her some, but she was just more careful around them now.

"Are you going to be around all the time then?" she tried to joke.

"I think I might just have to be."

He gave her a soft kiss that just grazed over her mouth. It wasn't a kiss about heat, it was something else. It almost felt like a promise.

Luna came from a mindset of practicality. Nobody made promises without getting something back. Strangers certainly didn't make promises, not that she was a hundred percent sure that Ford was still a stranger. She figured that making out with someone in public moved them out of casual acquaintance group.

"My girls are going to give me an earful about this," she said to herself but it was aloud.

"Your girls?"

Luna started walking and told him about the group of women that had helped saved her life. She hadn't really shared this much with anyone that she hadn't already known for a while. There was something that told her Ford wouldn't think she was less because she had sought out others that had suffered a loss like her.

She told him how they had wrapped her up in understanding and support at a time that she so desperately needed it. That without them she wouldn't be where she was today.

"I'd like to meet these women. They sound like my sisters and my brothers' wives. An amazing, yet slightly terrifying, tribe."

"That's what they are. My tribe. You know how they say it takes a village to raise a child? Well, it takes a tribe of women to keep a single woman from drowning."

"I think they've done a great job."

Luna had to hold back a tear. "They really have. If you can have a dozen women be your soul mates, then they are definitely my soul mates."

"I think they can be whatever you want them to be."

They walked a little while longer talking and

looking at the vendors selling everything imaginable or 'as seen on TV.'

"Time for games?" He asked when they had made it through the building.

"Sure, I love throwing money away."

CHAPTER 12

A few hours later, they were walking back to his car carrying a large stuffed monkey and two small bags containing goldfish.

"I need to name them. What's a good name for a fish?"

"I don't know. They aren't like cats and dogs you know. They need people names."

"People names?"

"Sure, like Fred the Fish or Barry."

"Nobody names their fish Barry."

"Maybe they should. Or Carl, that's a strong fish name."

"I knew you had to have a flaw. It's naming pets," she said with a giggle.

"Fine then, what are you going to name them?"

Luna pretended to ponder her options. "Peyton and Eli," she said proudly.

"Football fan, huh? I can respect that."

"Can't help it, they both are goofy and adorable. My fishes are goofy and adorable. It fits."

"Then let's go get Peyton and Eli a new home."

Ford drove them to the local pet store and they picked out a small tank, and she found an appropriately sized ceramic house and a small goal post for them in case they wanted to toss the ball around. Grabbing the rest of the necessary items to keep her fish alive, they checked out and headed back to the truck.

"Thanks for letting me pay for my own fish tank," she quipped.

"I didn't like it. I feel like I should be paying fish support or something since I won them for you."

"Fish support? Hah! They will be fine and happy being supported by a single mother, thank you."

Once they were settled in the truck it got quiet and Luna bit her lip as she tried to think of how to end the night.

"So..." she started.

"Luna..."

"I guess you can drop me back at the salon."

"I don't want to."

Luna wasn't sure what she wanted. She knew she didn't want to go home alone. But then the alternative was a daunting idea that made her think about finding her medicine in the bottom of her purse.

Since she wasn't sure what she wanted, she copped out and asked him. "What do you want?"

"You know. I told you earlier. I want to find a nice soft bed and spend the night making love to you."

"Who says that?"

"Honest men. I'm honest. I want you. It's simple."

"But what does that mean for me? A one-night stand?"

"No. But what if it was? A night with me, where I promise you'll leave happy. You're an adult; you can make those decisions yourself."

Luna felt that ache in her stomach that always started when all of her doubts and uncertainties would rise up and make her think negative things about herself.

"What if *you* don't leave happy?"

There was a look of shock and confusion on his face, and then there was a hint of annoyance. "How the fuck am I not going to leave happy?"

"I'm just saying, it's because..."

"Because what?"

"You know my history. What if I'm not good in bed? I didn't even know my husband was gay. Shouldn't I have known? Maybe I'm so bad that I didn't know I was doing it wrong."

He was quiet for a moment. She could see his mind working behind his eyes. "You've never been with anyone but your ex?"

"No."

"Luna, I'm a little shocked. I'm just trying to figure out how the hell you got that idea."

"Uh, have you met my ex?"

"Yes. And he may love you, which I could tell that he did. But, honey, he wasn't attracted to you. Not because you aren't beautiful, because you are. And it wasn't because you weren't good in bed. It's just who he is. It's like eating ice cream because it tastes good and knowing you're lactose intolerant. It's never gonna work. Did you ever think that maybe you weren't the one lacking in the bedroom?"

"Him? But he... you know, could do it."

"Just you saying 'do it' makes me think that there was very little passion involved."

No, Luna couldn't say there was ever any passion. It was always just... nice.

"I'm not sure I'd know what passion was. I figured that we had an okay relationship when it came to that. It seemed like married women were always complaining about stuff like that."

"That's on television. It's a running joke. Real live women that are well taken care of don't complain. The women in my life are very open about their love lives. They demand a certain level of satisfaction, and if it's not met there is hell to pay."

"I don't know women like that. Well, maybe Cambry. She's in a new relationship and seems pretty happy. They do it, like all the time."

"You're supposed to want to do it all the time. It's fun and feels good. Normally when something is good and fun, you want to do it more often. Haven't you ever just gotten so wound up that you have to come just to think straight?"

"Wow, no. I mean I used to want sex all the time, but I was younger. I guess I just got used to getting it a few times a year. If I took care of myself, you know...."

"I know."

"Then I wanted it more. And it wasn't something I wanted to have to ask for so I just pushed it out of my life. I was happy. Don't get me wrong. It was just a quiet sort of life."

Luna couldn't believe she had just shared all that with him. In the light of day, she was going to have a hard time looking him in the eye.

He had been quiet as he listened to her. His face had gone from confused and annoyed to an expression she couldn't read.

"I guess that makes me sound like a loser or something." She shouldn't have said that. Those shitty feelings she'd spent so many months working on tamping down were resurfacing.

Ford's eyes flashed to hers. "You are not a loser."

He put the car into gear and started driving. He seemed to know where he was going and she expected him to just take her back to the salon. Her overshare had probably made him want to roll her out at the nearest gas station to get away from her.

They came up to the turn for her shop and he got on the freeway instead.

"My salon is the other way, Ford."

"Oh, there is no way I'm dropping you off there with you thinking shit like that."

"Shit? What shit? Now you made me say shit!"

"Just the fact that you can't hear yourself makes me crazy. You've been settling for less than you deserve for years and that ends tonight. I'm taking you to my place. I'm going to show you what you've been missing."

Luna was a little shocked at the turn of events. She really thought unloading on him would make him run. A small part of her was using it as a defense mechanism. She wouldn't have to face the truth if she kept people at arm's reach.

"Do I get a say in this?"

"You have all the say in this. Just think back to that first kiss, or even the second. Remember how that felt?"

Luna did remember. It was a moment that was burned into her mind now. She'd use it in the future to compare her feelings to. In those moments, she felt like she was fully awake.

"I remember."

"That's passion, Luna. Real, honest to goodness passion. It tells me that we are going to be good together. Better than good. There is a very good chance we will be fucking fantastic. I think you deserve that and even if I don't deserve it, I sure as hell want it."

Go home with him? Have S-E-X with him? Just because she wanted to? The embarrassment level that was trying to register in her mind broke. Luna wanted to text her friends, get their opinions. She hadn't made any real life choices without them since she had joined their group. But they couldn't make this decision for her. It was hers to make and she was terrified to make it.

She liked him. He was handsome, sweet, and funny. He liked her, he'd said he did. Several times now. He almost seemed proud to be with her when they were walking around the fair. He protected her and coddled her. It had been a few hours where Luna didn't feel like she was on her own in the big world and some of the weight of her life had been lifted by some good food, some fun, and a great man.

"I'm nervous. I don't know what I should do."

"I'll tell you what I think. This part, this moment right now. This is the hard part. It's the most vulnerable you are ever going to be with me. After this moment, it gets better. It will get easier. So easy that when you're with me, you won't even have to think about it. I can promise you that."

"You can make that kind of promise?"

"It's like pulling off a band-aid. The waiting and deciding when to rip it off can be worse than the actual pain. Go ahead and make the leap, see how much better you feel."

"You're good with words, Ford. Too good. I haven't even been tempted until I met you."

"I'll take that as a compliment. Just say yes and then we'll face the next steps together."

Together. She liked the way that sounded. A partner, someone by her side. Someone to share her life with. True, Ford wasn't promising the future. Maybe she didn't need that from him. Maybe she just needed the right now. If she could get through a relationship with Ford, maybe the next one would be even easier, and someday she might find the one.

She didn't think Ford could be the one. He was too good. Too perfect for her. She needed someone with a few more dings so she wouldn't ever feel that she wasn't good enough for them. Luna didn't need to explain that to Ford. She'd just keep that to herself.

"I like you. I do. Can you just promise me something?"

"Anything."

"If you don't like me after... just tell me you had a good time and that you'll call me. When you don't call, I'll know and we won't have to hash it out. I'll get it."

"Fuck me, Luna. We have got to work on your self-esteem. I see that it's going to take a little more work on my part. Lucky for you, I like a challenge."

Luna shrugged. "Like I said, just say you'll call me and I'll understand."

She heard a growling noise from him and saw his hand flex on the steering wheel. Luna wasn't trying to be difficult; she was just giving them both an exit strategy. It seemed like a good idea.

CHAPTER 13

Ford wasn't angry at Luna. He was mad at the world and sad as shit for her. Someone so amazing shouldn't feel the way she did about herself. How could she not look in the mirror every morning and see that she was a force to be reckoned with?

"Who hurt you?"

He heard her make a little noise.

"Who?"

"Who was it that broke your heart?"

She was quiet for a moment. "Me."

Fuck him. Ford wasn't prepared for that. He needed a dragon to slay. His inner caveman was pounding his chest and looking to swing his club.

"Sorry?"

"I broke my own heart. I didn't protect it. I didn't face the reality that was in front of me and I let things go on for way too long. I let those around me, namely Al's family, tear me down because I thought they had a right to. I know now they didn't, but I still allowed it to happen. I blamed myself for wasted years of living with a man that didn't love me like he said he did. I knew it. I did. Deep down you know when someone says one thing but feels something else. I allowed my heart to be broken because I wanted my marriage to look as normal as everyone else's."

Ford took that in. He wanted to be angry with her ex, but he had been doing the same things she was blaming herself for. His family, that was something else to delve into. Why anyone would blame her for the failure of that marriage was ridiculous.

"I'm not sure you are to blame for everything," he started softly. "I believe that whenever a relationship ends it's good to look over it and see if there was something you could learn from it. I don't know all your details but it sounds like you may be taking on too much of the blame for this. Your ex knew who he was and kept that from you and everyone else. Don't shoulder all of it because others are blaming you."

She was silent on that and he knew that shield was going to have to be breached. "No more heavy talk tonight unless you really want to. We'll save if for a rainy day, yeah?"

Luna nodded and looked down at the fish that were in her lap swimming around in a tiny plastic container. He thought back to when she was so happy they weren't in little bags. It scared her she said.

So cautious and afraid. And it wasn't a fear of being hurt or of the unknown, that was what you were designed to be afraid of. It was as if she was afraid of failing at anything. Even in transporting some fish home.

Ford was going to have to set up opportunities for her to win. Even if he had to make a daily event to get her to see herself like he did.

Luna was leaning over the counter at Ford's condo, her head resting in her hands as she watched Peyton and Eli swimming happily around their new tank. Ford had shown her how to make sure the water temperature was right and to test the Ph to make sure it would work for them. They rinsed all the rocks and new toys and greenery she'd got and set up their tank.

She showed them their new home and gave them some food. They seemed happy with their roomy new place. Peyton was checking out the little house while Eli kept booping against the glass as though he was looking for a way out.

After their talk in the car, Luna's mind had been spinning. When he'd asked her who had hurt her, even she was shocked that her mind hadn't immediately blamed Al. Instead, she answered without thinking. There was a definite sense of shame that she had let herself down. Maybe it was the therapy, maybe it was just time, but there was a part of her that was mad at herself for getting into the place that she had fallen. Sure, she could have denied her feelings and kept on as she had been. Instead, the post-divorce emotional explosion had left a crater she had to dig herself out of. If she hadn't fallen where she did, would she be in a better place now? She wasn't so sure of that.

Now she was at Ford's house and her heart was racing. It had been a few years since she'd had sex. There just hadn't been any opportunities up until now. What if she forgot how? Or how she did it was wrong? Paranoia was setting in.

Ford had excused himself after they had set up the fish tank. She wasn't sure where he had gone. The urge to snoop around was high, so she stayed in the kitchen and talked to the fish.

She was holding back on contacting the girls. Her initial thought in the car was right. This was her decision and her call. Luna already knew what they were going to say. It would be a resounding chorus of "Go get some, girl!"

Just thinking about Ford like that made her want to wiggle. She wasn't lying about just not thinking about it. Once that part of her brain was turned off, it was surprising how long she had just done without and not noticed.

Now that part had been turned on, literally. She was experiencing a level of horniness that was unknown to her. Even if her brain could convince her to leave, her lady parts might stage a protest.

The image of tiny picket signs flashed through her mind and she giggled.

"They already doing tricks or telling jokes?"

"Oh no, just thought of something funny."

Ford came up behind her and pressed his body against hers. His hands resting on either side of the counter in front of her.

"Can I show you something?"

Luna nodded and he took her hand and walked her down the hallway. She knew it was his bedroom and her heart started pounding. Part of her wanted to run and the other part wanted to know what would happen once they stepped inside.

He walked her into his room. It wasn't anything fancy. It was almost set up like hotel room, or a room that he'd picked out of a furniture shop. The bed took up most of the room and there was a small light on beside the bed.

Luna took a ragged breath and decided in that moment that she was making the choice to spend the night with Ford. She was at peace with her decision if she wasn't a hundred percent settled on it. There was a chance she may never be totally comfortable. Still, it was a chance to make a decision on her own and to give herself the permission to move on.

"Nice, bed," she said, her voice catching.

"It is, very comfy. But that isn't what I wanted to show you."

Ford moved to another door that he pushed opened. As they walked in, she noticed the lights were turned off but there was a warm glow from candles reflecting off the mirror where they were sitting on the counter.

Opposite the counter was a large deep tub that was full and steaming. A layer of frothy bubbles rested on top.

"What is this?"

"This is for you. I want you to relax in this tub. Enjoy it and don't worry about anything. Take your time; I'll be in the living room."

"And when I'm done?"

"You can either call me in and I'll help you out. Towel you off and we can see what happens next. Or you can finish, get redressed and meet in the living room. We'll eat brownies and watch TV."

"That's all?"

"Why not? It's not what I want to do, but I still get to be with you, and that's not a bad way to end the evening in my book."

Luna was still holding his hand from when he had led her into the bathroom. He was too nice to be real. His sweetness and consideration was not what she was used to at all. Her ex had been thoughtful, but with a different feel to it.

"Okay, thank you."

"Thank you for what? It's just a bath."

"It's not just a bath. You know that."

Ford leaned towards her and placed a kiss on her forehead. "Relax."

He walked out of room and left her alone in the warm dark room.

CHAPTER 14

Ford was sitting on the couch. It was taking everything in him to not go and check on her. He wanted to see if she was enjoying herself. Whether or not she needed anything, whether her bath was still warm.

He didn't go; he wanted her to make the choices on her own. She had chosen to come to his house and for some that might be enough. But he knew that this was a bigger decision about herself than it was about him.

So he waited. He thought about how quickly his life could change for the better if she called for him. It would still change if she chose to come out and spend the rest of the evening on the couch with him. She might have been in there making some big choices, while Ford had been sitting there finalizing his own.

The minutes ticked by and he had started to

resign himself to the fact that he might have a quiet evening in store when he heard his name called out.

For a moment he thought it might have been his mind playing tricks on him. His hope so great that he'd heard her quiet voice call out his name.

Getting up, he walked by the kitchen and saw her phone was on the counter and the screen was lit. Picking it up to bring it to her, he saw the preview of the message in the notification bar. It just said, *Don't ruin another one...*

Ford didn't know what that meant; it wasn't any of his business. The message seemed vaguely hostile and he changed his mind about disturbing her bath. He'd ask her about it later.

He moved to his bedroom door and expected to go straight into bathroom. He stopped short when he saw Luna sitting on his bed, her hair tied into a large knot on top of her head. Instead of taking the towel he'd left for her and wrapping it around herself, she was holding it gently draped over the front of her. The hint of her shoulders and one arm that was clutching the towel. It lay over her lap leaving her legs exposed.

"Luna..." he said her name in a whisper. She was a vision that took his breath away.

"I'm here, Ford, because I want to be."

Ford didn't want to overthink this. He walked towards her and slowly started removing his clothing. It didn't seem fair that she wasn't dressed and he was.

Stripping down, he stood naked and let her look

her fill. Ford was proud of his body; he was strong for his job, but he wasn't unaware that he looked good. His body was trim, his chest was broad and flat, and his stomach rippled with lean muscle.

"Wow," she murmured.

"It's only fair. You look beautiful; I don't want you to think that I don't appreciate your gift."

"Gift?"

"Believe me, you sitting there is like Christmas morning."

A blush stole over her cheeks.

"That just makes you prettier."

Ford took a step closer then sat next to her. He brushed a lock of hair that had fallen from her bun behind her ear.

She was looking up at him with a look so deep and unfathomable that he was momentarily lost in her gaze. He could spend the rest of his life looking into those blue eyes and die a happy man.

"You're perfect," he said to her, moving his thumb over her lower lip.

"I'm not," she whispered back.

"You are for me."

Ford kissed her then, slowly, but made sure she knew that he was exactly where he wanted to be. It was slow and he didn't want to rush her. Her skin was soft and she smelled of the bath and bubbles.

He shifted so he was lying on the bed and pulled her down with him.

CHAPTER 15

Luna gasped as their naked bodies connected. It was something she had missed so much. That skin on skin contact was something she hadn't realized was so important. His skin was warm and strong and with his arms around her, she felt like there wasn't anything in the world that could get into that room. There was nothing that could get between them.

There was a little voice in her head that kept telling her that this wouldn't last. That he'd get tired of her. That there was something inherently wrong about her that a man wouldn't want to be with her long term.

So if she couldn't have him forever, she'd have him for as long as she could. Ford made her heart feel better. Like some of the spaces that had cracked open a few years ago were starting to heal. Maybe even after Ford was gone, those wounds wouldn't reopen.

She chose to let her mind slip back and give way

to her body. Her skin felt like it was lighting up and coming alive.

"Luna, Luna, you are amazing," he said into her ear.

It was almost easy to believe when he said it. She wished she could take that feeling home with her. For now, she would enjoy it.

"It's been a while, for me. Just so you know. I may not be very good at this."

"Oh darlin', what makes you think that?"

"I don't have any reason to think otherwise."

"I'll make you a deal, after tonight, no more talk like that. I get where you're coming from. It would make anyone doubt themselves, but I know that you have nothing to worry about."

Luna liked that idea. Not worrying anymore. Not having that nagging voice in her head telling her that no matter what she had accomplished it wasn't enough.

Ford started kissing her. She hesitated for a moment and he seemed to kiss her deeper so she relaxed. If nothing else, she wanted him to feel good too. This wasn't just about her. It was about them. For as long as there was a 'them.'

His hands roamed over her and she wanted to try and experience all of it, every touch, every skim of his fingers, but it was overwhelming. Her body arched up to his touch without her even thinking about it. He was confident and sure of his movement.

Luna used her hands to move over his chest. His

muscles were hard and she'd never felt muscles like that. Seeing them and feeling them were different. She moved her hands over his arms, feeling his biceps. She decided to be bold and skimmed her fingers over his chest.

"Luna, my Luna. How in the world did I get so lucky?"

"If anyone is lucky it's me. I'm afraid to like you because I don't want to miss you."

Telling him that opened her up to all sorts of emotional danger. Luna shouldn't have said it, but now it was out there.

"I won't give you a chance to miss me."

～

Luna didn't know how long they had been in his bedroom. She had tried to keep up with Ford and wasn't able to. He had her spiraling so out of control that she wasn't even sure if she was participating anymore. All she could do was feel. And she did. It was amazing, her body was on fire. He touched her; he tormented her. His hand was between her legs, and he was teasing her so mercilessly. It was brilliant.

She was being greedy and wanted to remember everything. The truth was she would be lucky to be able to recall much of the evening.

"Ford, I don't know if I can."

"Of course you can. In fact, I demand it. Luna, come for me."

Luna wasn't sure if she could, she was holding back and she knew it. When Ford told her he was expecting it... demanding it, she felt a release of a different sort. She didn't need to restrain herself; she didn't need to hold it all together anymore.

The building pressure that had built inside her, the aching pleasure that had risen to a peak tumbled out of her. Luna let out a mewling cry as she clutched Ford's arm. Luna in another life would never have come yelling and panting. Her previous experiences had been restrained and quiet, polite even. There was no politeness now. It was like a dam had broken inside her and her pleasure had her only seeing stars behind her eyelids. Her body was locked and grasping at every sharp bite of pleasure.

Normally she'd be dying of embarrassment. Not this time. It was wonderful and she couldn't bring herself to put anything bad on it.

As her thought processes slipped back, she was going to think of some witty quip to say to bridge the awkwardness. She heard the rip of a condom wrapper then Ford was moving into her with a slow steady thrust that made her brain misfire. He wasn't being fast or rough, it was just a claiming of body and soul that she had to catch up with.

He stopped and waited for her. She appreciated that.

"Luna, let me see your eyes."

Luna opened her eyes and saw him over her. He

was so handsome, and he was smiling down at her, and she wasn't expecting that.

"Watch me. I'm here, with you, and no one else."

He started to move and Luna was so caught up that she pushed what he had said to the back of her mind. She'd have to decipher it later.

Ford made love to her. It wasn't fast and it wasn't with the sole intent of him getting off. He took his time and made her burn.

CHAPTER 16

Ford lay with Luna in his arms. He knew that she was pretending to be asleep and he let her have that. He was content with her the way they were, and he was sure there was a lot going on in her mind. Every time she said something negative about herself, his first reaction was to pummel whoever it was that had put those thoughts in her head in the first place. His second response was sadness that a woman as bright and loving as she was would ever think poorly about herself.

If he could have picked out all the things he enjoyed in a lover, Luna would match every one. She was giving, she touched and kissed him, and then she enjoyed what he had to offer her. That decadent decision to let someone else please you did wonderful things for his ego. And please her he had. He made her come over and over, testing and memorizing her likes and dislikes. He wanted to learn everything there was to keep Luna happy and at his side.

He knew he had some convincing to do, but now after having her, the task of winning over Luna Kind had become immensely more pleasurable. Cuddling her closer, their sweaty bodies touching shoulder to toe, he let his eyes drift close and made plans on how he was going to wake her up in the morning.

Luna was waiting for Ford to go to sleep. She didn't want to talk to him, or maybe she did. Did he want her to leave? Or stay? He was wrapped pretty tightly around her. She guessed that if he had wanted her to leave, he would have distanced himself. Rolled over and ignored her. Instead, he was holding on to her like he'd drown if he didn't.

With her limited experience, he seemed to have enjoyed himself. She knew she did and she couldn't wait to tell the girls. Ford talked during sex. He commented, described and kept up a constant chatter while they made love. Luna wasn't a big talker so she hoped that he wasn't offended when she kept her responses limited to gasps and moans. The chances of her actually forming words had been slim to none.

If she weren't so worried about what came next she'd give herself a moment to relax and enjoy the aftermath. But she was analyzing. Her therapist would tell her that she was missing the moment.

As Scarlett O'Hara would say, tomorrow is another day. Luna did have tomorrow and she needed to be the strong woman everyone said she was and handle whatever came next, good or bad. Her heart was feeling a little tender, in a good way. She liked Ford. He was a balm to the rough edges of her heart. She was afraid of getting used to that sensation. There was no way she'd miss it when it was gone.

Settling in, she started counting her breaths, hoping she would fall asleep and not snore.

As it turned out, she didn't snore. At least Ford didn't mention that she had. Not that he was very talkative when they woke up. Luna was having the most delicious dream and it was full of naughty things that she and Ford could do.

She woke up to Ford expertly acting out one of those dream sequences between her legs. Compared to last night he was shockingly quiet, then again, talking would have been difficult.

Luna had never woken up to a screaming orgasm in her life and she had to say, it was better than coffee.

Ford had slid into her while she was still coming down and had made passionate love to her. He then switched gears and jumped up pulling her into the bathroom and into the shower where he proceeded to scrub her down from head to toe.

Luna tried to protest and he scolded her playfully for taking away his fun.

"Luna, let me enjoy myself. I assure you I'll do an adequate job."

He did more than that, and he somehow turned the act of getting clean into something much more decadent.

Ford was able to get dressed much quicker than her, and he pointed out the hairdryer for her to use. When she came out into the kitchen, she saw him setting a plate out on the long bar. She pulled out a stool and Ford put a cup of coffee next to her plate.

"Eggs and bacon? Do you always eat like this?"

"I like my protein. Don't you eat this for breakfast?"

"Yes, when I'm with my friends at IHOP. Otherwise I'm a yogurt and cereal girl."

"Today, I get to feed you. Peyton and Eli have been fed. I was thinking we could take them to your salon this morning. I'm on shift at noon; I don't know when I'll be able to call you."

There it was, his brush off. She could take this. She was an adult, no need to get wishy-washy about it."

"That's fine. I'm sure I'll see you around," she said, trying to act casual.

"See me around? Just when do you think you'll be seeing me around?"

"Oh, you know, whenever?" she offered with a shrug.

Ford came around the counter and took a seat next to her, he turned her stool so it was facing him and pulled her face to his to give her a kiss that was not appropriate for the breakfast table.

"You will be hearing from me. I'll text you when I can, and I'll call when I can. Tomorrow night we can come back here and I'll cook you fettuccine and we'll see if we can break our record from last night. I do love a challenge."

Luna's heart skipped a beat. He wanted to see her again. He wanted to keep in touch with her. He wanted to have sex with her again! These were all reasons for her to squeal and she had to restrain herself.

"Okay," she managed.

"Okay. You and I? We're a team. This is happening. After last night, let's just say that if I didn't have to work I wouldn't let you out of my sight. Unfortunately, I do have to work and I hope you understand that it's my job and I can't change it. That doesn't mean you aren't my priority now. We will work this out."

"Ford, I know you love your job. I would never want to get in the way of that. I'm not the type that would do that. I..."

"You what?"

"I just feel like you should know. I don't think I'm good enough for you, and I know that it can be annoying to have to constantly reassure someone. It's a full-time job and I'll try really hard to not annoy you."

"Luna, you couldn't annoy me if you tried. And believe it or not, I see your pain. You've had a tough run and I'm going to get you to the other side. I'm going to get you to understand that you are a prize to any man. I'm not trying to make it sound like you are someone to be won, but there are plenty of men that think that way. You are a prize, and I sure as hell will be proud to have you on my arm. There is no reason for you to think you aren't worthy. There isn't anything about you I'd change. So, if you tell me that you aren't the one for me then you're saying that I don't want the best. I do, I want the best, and that's you."

Luna wanted to believe him. It would be an amazing thing to have a man devoted to her. One that liked her for everything she was. The previous night showed her what passion was. True passion. Not just for the physical, but that burning desire to be close to someone. Luna felt like her breath came easier when Ford was with her. Her desire to hold it together was barely a thought, because he so easily enveloped her in a world of his own making. She liked his world, it was nice, it was pleasurable, and his ability to encourage her and bolster her confidence was exactly what she needed.

"I'll try to be present. I want to be. I don't want

to feel bad anymore. I can't promise I won't slip. I've been doing it for a while."

"Then I'll be here to remind you that you are worth it."

For the first time in a long time, she wanted to be worth it for him.

"Also, it may not be any of my business, but you got a message last night. It didn't seem like a pleasant one so I didn't want to disturb your bath. This morning again, you're phone chimed and the preview just said, bitch in capital letters. Something you want to tell me?"

"Not really?"

"Luna, is someone bothering you? You know I'm here for you. I do know a lot of people in the police department, hell, they're family."

"No, no police. It's just... it's Alton's family."

"Alton's family is calling you a bitch? Why the fuck for?"

"They didn't take our divorce very well. They haven't talked to Alton since it happened and they found out about why we split up. They're unhappy and they needed someone to take it out on."

Ford's face was starting to turn a scary shade of red. "And you decided to be the sacrificial lamb and take their shit?"

"It's not like it matters. They just text me, sometimes they call and leave a voicemail. I just delete them. It gives them an outlet."

"Babe, they need to go to therapy if they need an

outlet. They don't need to be abusing you. Shit this has been going on for years hasn't it?"

Luna shrugged. "It's really not a big deal."

"Luna, my Luna, it's a big fucking deal. But I want you to have a good day. So I'm going to kiss the hell out of you and make sure you have that blurry, happy look in your eyes before I send you off to work. We'll talk about this bullshit later."

Luna didn't want to talk about it. She'd found a tolerance for it and didn't see the need to rock the boat. It probably wasn't going to be what Ford wanted to hear, so she kept it to herself.

"Okay," she said, ending the conversation hopefully for good.

CHAPTER 17

Luna was riding on a high. Ford had taken her and her fish to the salon and she almost fainted when he laid a kiss on her so hot she thought she would melt through the floor.

"I'll text, and or call you. Promise."

She nodded and waved him out the door. Luna set her fish up in the break room and stowed her purse. Picking up her phone she typed out a text that she knew would get her girls riled up.

Luna: Can you have too many orgasms?
Elena: This is what I wake up to?!
Waverly: I'm so proud.
Cambry: No, medically it's not possible.
Evie: Shut up!
Luna: He's...amazing.
Evie: Sounds like it!

Waverly: Were you safe? You know nothing sours a new relationship like an STD.

Cambry: Don't listen to her, she's grumpy from lack of orgasms.

Waverly: True, but you can bite me.

Luna: He wants to see me again. He said he would call me while he's at work and wants me to come over tomorrow night.

Elena: That sounds like a happy man.

Luna: I want to make him happy. It's weird. He makes me feel good and I want to return the favor.

Evie: Then do it. Be happy crazy girl!

Luna: I feel weird. I have to face Alton this morning.

Cambry: No offense honey, but he's been getting some regular. I don't think you need to worry about jealousy.

Evie: That's graphic.

Waverly: Sounds sexy. He'll be happy for you. He's a good guy.

Luna: I got a text last night. Al's mom. She's still so angry. I feel bad for her.

Cambry: Oh, that shit has to stop. Fuck them. Be happy. They need to figure their own shit out.

Elena: I second that statement.

Luna: I know I should. I just feel like I failed them.

Elena: You didn't.

Cambry: You didn't.

Waverly: You didn't.

Evie: You didn't, they're being stupid and hateful. Banish them and move on.

Luna: Thanks guys, I gotta get to work. I'll let you know if he texts.

Luna was abandoning the chat because she knew they were right. It was like her one last penance that she couldn't let go of. A little part of her hoped that letting them vent at her would give them a chance to heal.

The truth was; hate never bred love.

The rest of her day was busy. She was fitting in walk-ins during her regular appointments and it had her running around like a crazy woman.

Sometime in the afternoon, she got a phone call and thinking it might be Ford, she grabbed it and hit accept without thinking.

"Hello?"

"You bitch! You think you can ruin another man's life? You should be ashamed of yourself. I can't stand to think of what you did to my brother. This isn't over, you stupid cow."

Luna stopped in her tracks and was standing in the middle of the salon holding her phone to her ear. It had been a while since she'd gotten a full on verbal attack. They had resorted to just the text messages a while ago. Since her defenses were down, the words hit her like gunshot. What if she did ruin Ford? What if this was her fault, something she did or didn't do? Ford was too great of a guy to have his life derailed.

She was just being greedy. Wanting something she

couldn't have. There wasn't any way to know if she could make Ford happy. They could spend weeks or months trying and they would both come out of it worse for the wear. Alton's sister was right. She shouldn't risk Ford to the unknown. He needed someone that was undamaged. Someone that could just be with him without all her stupid hang-ups. What kind of man would want a woman that came with her own set of luggage? Her baggage was varied and packed full.

Tucking the phone back in her pocket, she felt herself slip into autopilot. Walking back to the break room, she found her purse, dug into the bottom and took out her anxiety medication. She slid a pill into her mouth and got back to her life.

An hour later, she got a text from Ford.

Ford: Miss you, hope your day is going good.

She ignored it. There was nothing to say to him. He was probably having a great day. Washing firetrucks and playing foosball with his pals. Or he was rescuing kittens from trees. Either way, he had a life that didn't need her in it.

Another text buzzed and she left her phone in her pocket this time. The next few buzzes she ignored as well. Larissa came around the corner at some point bouncing on her toes.

"You have a call. I think it's that hottie."

"Tell him I'll have to call him back," she murmured as she focused on her client's hair.

She saw Larissa's confused expression as she

turned back to the reception desk but had to let that go.

Focusing on work was all she could do. Her medication had kicked in and she had a slight tingling sensation that was coursing through her that immediately slowed her heart rate and gave her those extra seconds she needed to control her emotions. It was numbing, but sometimes it was worth not feeling.

CHAPTER 18

"Toby? Can I get Alton's number?"

"Yeah man, everything okay?"

"No, Luna isn't answering any of my texts."

"A little possessive are you? One date and you have your caveman stick out?"

"She got a text last night from someone named Susan? It wasn't nice. I'm worried that the message got to her."

"That bitch! Damnit, I didn't know they were still talking to her! Alton hasn't said anything."

Ford shook his head. "I'm guessing he doesn't know. I think this has been going on for a while. Like a nasty little devil on her shoulder picking away at her self-esteem."

"Alton's family didn't take their divorce well. And since they wouldn't accept him, he told them not to call him until they did. I guess he should have put Luna on that do not call list."

"Yeah, she's been taking their abuse this whole time. It stops today."

"Agreed."

Toby gave him the number and Ford called Alton. His day had started so well. His happiness had been obvious when he got to work. His co-workers who were like family could see the change in him immediately. They gave him a ribbing about it and then they would slap him on the back and give him the chin lift that told him they were happy for him.

One of his coworkers, Margie, came up to him and stared hard at him for a while. Then she said, "Don't fuck this up."

"I don't intend on it." She gave him a punch in the arm and then joined the crew on the couches where they were watching a movie.

He had expected a response to his texts. The first one he wrote off to her being busy. The second and third he figured maybe she left her phone in her purse somewhere. Then he started to get worried. She had seemed happy during breakfast. He thought their night together had been good. As far as he was concerned, it had been fantastic and he was eager to repeat the entire evening. Fish included.

His worry got the best of him and he called the salon. When she wouldn't take his call, he knew something was up.

Calling Alton might seem like he was going behind her back, but it was *his* family and he needed to handle it.

"Hello?"

"Alton, it's Ford."

"Hey! I feel special getting phone calls from you now. How did you get my number?"

"Called Toby. I need to talk to you about something serious."

"If you're asking for Luna's hand in marriage that will be a no. Too soon."

"No, it's not that and I wouldn't ask you anyway. I've been trying to get a hold of her all day and she's ignoring me. I think I know why. Did you know she's been getting calls from your family? Nasty text messages and there were at least three unheard voicemails on her phone. I wasn't snooping I saw it on the counter last night."

"Fucking hell! You have got to be shitting me. It's been two years. Two fucking years!"

Alton was losing his shit and Ford was more than a little happy with his response. He wanted Alton to get pissed enough to fix it for good.

"I haven't heard shit from my family since the divorce. Not one single word, not a card, not one text, nothing. And they've been abusing Luna this whole time? And she didn't tell me?"

"I can't say I know her as well as you do, but it's Luna. She'd take the hits to protect you, wouldn't she?"

"Shit, she would. She always did. That heart of hers would set itself on fire if it meant protecting someone else."

"Alton, this may sound weird, but I like Luna. Hell, if you believe in love at first sight, then I'm that too. This woman stole my heart in a big way. I won't let anyone hurt her. I'm giving you first go to deal with this because it's your family. If it doesn't stop, I'll rain holy hell down on them for torturing her all these years."

"I do believe in love at first sight. I know that punch in the gut that takes your breath away and makes your heart heavy in your chest. If you feel that for Luna, then I'm a happy man. She deserves that. I'll take care of the family. I'm afraid you are going to have to fix the damage. She's all yours now."

"I got Luna covered. You just get that shit to stop."

"Consider it done."

CHAPTER 19

Luna was in a nice hazy place. Her last few appointments had been easy enough that she could coast on autopilot. It was so strange on her medication. She still thought about the things that were bothering her, the things that scared or hurt her, but those thoughts didn't have a physical response. No anxious feeling, no struggle to breathe.

She had forgotten how relaxing it could be to not have to feel everything. She could think about Ford and not worry about wanting him, physically or otherwise. It was for the best that she didn't call him back. Their night together had been great and she'd always have the memory of it. Ford wouldn't have to be involved in her messy life and she could become a crazy fish lady since she didn't have time for cats.

Taking the cape off her last client, she walked her to the front and said goodbye. When she got back to her station, she saw Alton leaning against her counter.

"Hey my phone died, can I borrow yours to look something up? There is a new restaurant I want to try."

"Sure, here," she said, pulling her phone from her pocket. A little bell was ringing in her head that told her that she should have checked her messages before handing it over. But he was just using the internet.

Alton stared at her phone for a while. She tidied up around him, sweeping up hair and picking up products. She went to the back to throw her towels in the wash and when she came back, Alton was staring at her, a frown marring his normally handsome face.

"What?"

He stared for a moment, his arms crossed and his brow furrowed.

"Take a seat," he said gesturing towards her chair.

Luna sat down and gave him her own frown. "What?"

"Luna Kind you have officially gone from being kind-hearted to being a fucking idiot."

"Ouch, that's mean," she said.

"First, did you take your meds today? I can see that glassy look in your eyes."

"Maybe, they're mine to take when I need them, what do you care?"

"I care because they make you a robot. You are

too wonderful to float through life like that. You were doing great without them and I know how tough it was for you to get to that place. Did you take one because of the message my sister sent?"

Shit. Shit. Shit! She should have cleared her messages. That little bell in her head was now ringing, *I told you so.*

"I just got a little overwhelmed. They help."

"I know they do, sweetie. But I can't decide whether I'm pissed at you or not for not telling me about these messages. Luna, they have no right to talk to you this way. You've been taking this abuse for years, what were you thinking?"

"I was thinking that they miss you, and they're mad. I get missing you and being mad. They needed to vent their anger at someone."

"No, they need to get over themselves and get on with their own damn lives. You are not their punching bag! If they have shit to say, they can say it to me. No one else. We know the truth of our relationship. We know the truth of our life together now. We don't need their approval or their understanding to live happily. You know good and well that our marriage wasn't the problem. My journey, for better or worse, got tangled with yours and I won't lie, I'm happy it did. I can't live my life without Luna Kind in it. You are my best friend and my life would be darker without you."

Luna still loved him. Now though, that love was different. It was friendship and camaraderie that she felt. Her heart was filling up with another man. One that she shouldn't feel so attached to after such a short time, but she couldn't help it. He was everything she could have hoped for and she was terrified to reach out and take it for herself.

"Here's what's going to happen. I have deleted all the messages and voicemails from my family. I have deleted their contacts and blocked all their numbers. You will not accept any calls or messages from unknown numbers from now on. I will be having Toby write up cease and desist notices for all my family with threat of having them charged with harassment and stalking because I don't know how the hell they found out about Ford. That shit is unacceptable. You, my darling, are going to answer that man's calls and tell him that you've missed him and that you can't wait to see him. I can see it even now in your eyes. You need him and from the call I had with him today, he needs you too."

"You talked to him?"

"He's a smart guy. He called Toby then called me. He likes you, sweetie. Hell, really, really likes you. Reel this hunk in, because he's hooked."

Luna could feel her meds wearing off because her heart was starting to beat faster. He cared enough to call her ex-husband to get someone to stop being mean to her. They'd been on one date. Granted that date had turned into a sleep over, but still he didn't owe her anything.

"I like him. I do. He makes me happy," she said quietly, tears starting to well in her eyes.

"Then jump into those big muscular arms and let him carry you away. He's a good one; I feel it in my bones. That man can happily handle anything that comes his way. And you are going to be the easiest one for him to take care of. Let him take care of you, and let him show you how to be happy again. Do it for yourself and no one else."

Luna felt a little guilt trickle in for ignoring him. He was good to her and she did miss him so much. She nodded at Alton as a single tear escaped and ran down her cheek.

He pulled her into his arms and gave her a big hug, lifting her off the ground.

"Put me down, you'll break something."

"Hah, I've been working out. You're lighter than a feather."

Luna made a choking noise. "Hardly. Thank you for your help, really. I have a hard time choosing between what is right and what I think others want. Your family is a bunch of... assholes," she said proudly.

"No, they are fucking assholes. Repeat after me please."

Luna gave him a look. "Fine, they are fucking assholes."

"Oh good, your therapist will be so proud. Now, go call your man."

CHAPTER 20

Luna tried calling Ford and got no answer. She sent him a text message apologizing for being rude and got no answer.

She decided she needed a grand gesture just in case he was unhappy with her. She needed to make amends for ignoring him.

After she got the address to his station from Toby, she stopped by the store and then parked outside the station and went to the entrance on the side. She pressed a buzzer by the door and waited.

"Yes? Can I help you?"

Leaning closer to the speaker she said, "Hi, um, I'm looking for Ford?"

"He's on a call. Probably about fifteen minutes out."

"Okay, I'll wait."

The speaker clicked dead and she went back to

her car and leaned against it. She was starting to feel a little silly standing there holding a Mylar balloon in the shape of a firetruck and a box with a giant pizza cookie. It had seemed cute and funny at the time but now she was feeling awkward.

It was almost thirty minutes later that two firetrucks pulled up to the driveway and men and women started pouring out of them all dressed in yellow bunker gear.

Squaring her shoulders and ignoring the horrible nauseating fear in her stomach, she stepped forward and looked for Ford.

She got some funny looks and more than a few smiles when she finally saw Ford coming around the front of one of the trucks.

"Luna?"

"Hey," she said, giving him a wonky smile.

His face, smeared with black soot and sweat broke into a grin. That feeling in her tummy lessened.

He walked up to her and gave her a kiss without saying anything. There were some hoots and whistles from behind him and she didn't care. He tasted like smoke and sweat and she couldn't have been happier.

"What are you doing here? Have you been waiting long?"

"I came to apologize for being rude. See?" she said, gesturing to the box.

Ford lifted the lid and started laughing. She had the cookie decorated with the words, *Sorry for ignoring you after sex*, in white icing. The look she got from the teenager at the cookie place nearly made her melt into a puddle of embarrassment, but she was trying to be bold.

"Baby, you don't need to apologize. I know you've had a tough run. I'm guessing Alton talked to you."

"Talked and yelled. But I know he did it out of love. I should have been stronger."

"Babe, you *are* strong. You just are too sweet to the wrong people."

"You're right, I am. Except when it comes to you. I want to be sweet to you. I like you, a lot. And even though it scares me, I don't want to lose you, Ford."

Ford took the cookie and set it on the ground so he could get closer to her. "Luna, you aren't going to lose me. I'm the luckiest man in the world that you want to be with me. I don't doubt how you feel and I don't want you to doubt me for a minute. I already told Alton what you meant to me and how serious I was. Do you think I'd say that to him if I didn't mean it? Call it what you want, but I need you, Luna. To the moon and back, I'm so happy I found you."

Luna wanted to hold back the tears but she couldn't as they fell on their own and she was happy her feelings were fully back. "I really, really like you too. Isn't that crazy? I can't think of anything else but being with you."

"Then we're both crazy, that works for me."

Ford kissed her and Luna soaked up all the love he put into it and gave it right back to him.

Luna couldn't believe that she and Ford had managed to make it to the four week mark before their first 'I love you's' were also their first pseudo fight.

"You know how I feel, Ford," she said standing against the counter in his apartment. They were getting ready for work and she had spent the night but didn't get much sleep.

"Yup, babe, I do. And you know how I feel. I'm one hundred percent certain of how I feel and what my future looks like. I'm just waiting for you to catch up."

"Catch up? What the hell do you think I've been doing for the last four weeks?"

"Stalling."

Luna felt a blood vessel start to pound in her forehead. "Stalling for what?"

"You're stalling because you're scared. I haven't pushed you because I already know how you feel. You just haven't figured it out for yourself yet."

"Oh, like you know me so freaking well. Well, maybe you don't. Maybe I've grown to hate you and I'm thinking of an escape plan!" Luna wasn't trying to escape, hell; she never wanted them to be apart. Even going to work was a little disappointing because it might mean that she wouldn't see him for a day or two while he was on shift.

Ford didn't say anything; he just raised one of those gorgeous eyebrows of his and waited.

"Fine, I fucking love you! Are you happy? I love you, Ford Jameson! Tell the world!" she said waving her arms around enthusiastically.

Ford watched her for a moment while she imitated a monkey on crack. Finally, he reached out, pulled her into his arms, and kissed her to stop the monkey noises coming out of her mouth.

Pulling away from her mouth, he kissed the tip of her nose. "I love you too, Luna Kind. I have from our first date. I just needed you to get there with me."

"I don't think I've ever really been in love with someone like this. It's kinda scary."

"It is. It's also the best feeling in the world."

~

Another month later

Waverly: Seriously, you can stop telling us every time you have amazing sex.
Cambry: Girl it's two in the morning.
Elena: Oh my god Becky, look at her butt!
Elena: Sorry wrong chat. Luna babe, it's been like two months.
Evie: I swear to god my phone chimes after midnight and I know it's a Luna fuck-update.
Luna: Hey, I just like you to know everything is going good.
Cambry: Bullshit you want to brag. Well I got some too, so there.

Luna: Actually tonight isn't about a sex brag. It's about something else.

Luna sent a picture of her hand sporting the ring that Ford had slid onto it a few hours before. They had been making love and Ford had rocked her world like he always did. She had collapsed on top of him afterward, which now she did regularly not worrying about if she was too heavy. She knew he happened to love it when she did it. She felt his hand come to her head and tilt it up so she could see him.

"I love you," he said.

She happily and dreamily replied, "I love you too."

"Are you ever going to leave me, Luna?"

"Where would I go?" she said with a laugh.

"I don't know, because there isn't a spot on this earth that I wouldn't travel to get you back."

"Good to know. I'd hate to go on vacation by myself."

"You know you're mine, now and forever."

Luna was used to these bold statements now. She adored them. Every word was a stone in the wall that kept her away from all the negativity that used to be in her life. She was safe, protected, and surrounded by an impenetrable fortress made up entirely of Ford's love.

"Always, Ford, forever."

"Let's go on vacation."

"Random, but okay. Where to?"

"Somewhere warm, somewhere I can enjoy seeing you in a bikini all day."

"Okay, when?"

"I'd say a few days after we are married?"

Luna pushed herself up on his chest. Ford was holding a beautiful ring in between his fingers.

"Luna Kind, will you marry me?"

Luna felt the last hole in her heart cement closed. She was stronger, more confident, and so proudly in love that she couldn't control herself.

"Yes!" She started laughing and crying at the same time as she kissed him. Ford had to wrestle her down to get the ring on her finger as she laughed and cried.

He made love to her again slowly and exquisitely. Luna didn't think her heart could get any bigger but it did. It swelled to bursting with her love for the man that had shown her that she was worth everything.

After he had slapped her on her ass and told her, "Go tell your girls."

He knew her so well.

Waverly: What?!
Elena: You had better said yes!
Cambry: Oh, sweetheart it's beautiful!
Evie: Oh, he went to Jared.
Gianna: Does he have a brother?
Paisley: Congratulation sweetheart!
Claire: If you didn't say yes, we are having you committed.
Dawn: He's a good one, I can tell.

Luna: He is the best. And yes, I said yes.

Luna had so many loves in her life now that she felt spoiled, but not spoiled rotten. She said good-night to her girls and slid back into bed with her man. Her man, who loved her for everything that she was, and everything she could be.

CONNECT WITH MICHELE

Thank you for for reading my story! There are more to come so be sure to sign up for my Newsletter or follow me on Facebook.

Subscribe to newsletter at: eepurl.com/cX2op1
New Releases, Giveaways, and More

facebook.com/authormichelebarlow

ALSO BY MICHELE BARLOW

THE BROKEN HEARTS CLUB
Loving Again
Starting Over
Breaking Free

Made in the USA
San Bernardino, CA
06 September 2017